The Protectors

The Protectors

WILLIAM HAGGARD

WALKER AND COMPANY
New York

First published in the United States of America in
1972 by the Walker Publishing Company, Inc.

ISBN: 0-8027-5262-4

Library of Congress Catalog Card Number: 72-80530

Printed in the United States of America

1

Mr James Scobell was far from happy for the feel of the business frightened him. He couldn't yet guess what the worst might be, but all diplomats scared him, especially rich ones, and this Peter van Ruyden was old Julius's grandson.

Scobell sighed softly and sent for tea. The morning drink of his country was washy coffee but he had served in England for fifteen years as the manager, he thought with a smile, of the Milton Export and Import Company. It was a front and those who mattered knew it, but nobody else would ever guess it. The Milton was a genuine business and genuinely paying its way. As for what lay behind the cover, James Scobell did his job with experienced competence. The orders which reached him he sometimes thought foolish, an over-reaction which years in England had taught him to mistrust profoundly, and sometimes he thought them absurdly irresolute. What was the point of enormous power if some eastern establishment liberal could block it? Why maintain his organization at all if some twinge of the national conscience could cripple it? Politicians would read opinion polls, politicians had private fences to mend. Only a handful were reliable realists and those didn't always come to the top.

Scobell sighed again but without resentment; he had been in England too long for that. He was the London head of an organization whose tentacles reached every country on earth but he thought of himself as a civil servant. The politicians made the big decisions, the administrators sorted them out. They did, that is, when they possibly could. He might even be able to sort out van Ruyden, though this, for good reasons, he rather doubted. Van Ruyden was both things he most mistrusted, a diplomat and an heir apparent. He was heir to a huge industrial empire, a survival from another time, the age of the great financial pirates.

Van Ruyden had taken an ordinary taxi, not the embassy car which he had at call, directing it to the house in Park Crescent. He climbed out briskly and paid the driver, savouring the district's aura. This was Good-Works-land, Councils for this cause, Committees for that. There was even an international Foundation. The people who staffed them were all of a type, men and women of the highest principle, but in their fashion they were also shrewd. There were salaries in this graceful Crescent which they couldn't have earned in the world outside it. What mattered here was solely service: profit and loss were dirty words. Peter van Ruyden despised these people but would have admitted that he and these tiresome shams had a single characteristic in common. Both of them were deeply dedicated, they to their absurd ideals, he to an end they'd have hated and feared. He supposed you could even call them civilized, a word which he didn't consider pejorative. He thought of himself as a civilized man and crude envy was threatening every value which he and his private background stood for.

Also its not inconsiderable privileges. Naturally one fought back at it fiercely.

Van Ruyden walked through a door up a flight of stairs.

2

On the landing there were other doors and on one of them a bright brass plate—*The Milton Export and Import Company*. When he pushed the door open he had crossed the Atlantic. The room he now stood in was decently warm, and if anyone drank tea there they had put away the cups and saucers. There were two clerks at business-like desks, a receptionist, and in a corner behind another desk a sharp-eyed young man in American shoes. The sharp-eyed young man looked van Ruyden over, then he smiled and said civilly :

'How can I help you?'

'I've an appointment with Mr James Scobell.'

'You're Mr van Ruyden? Yes, of course.' He bowed van Ruyden through another door which led into Scobell's private office.

Scobell had risen behind his desk. There was a writing-pad on it, a pen—nothing more. His hair was black, untouched by grey, though he must have been in his later fifties, and there was a hint of powder round a considerable but well-shaved jowl. He weighed two hundred pounds but was not yet flabby and he looked like the tackle he once had been.

James Scobell was as different from Peter van Ruyden as two men of the same race could be. Where van Ruyden talked eastern establishment Boston, Scobell had a fine western whine which it had never occurred to him to mitigate. His vocabulary, yes: on his last trip home they'd laughed at him. But never the whinny. He said in it now :

'Will you have a cigar?'

'I don't smoke, thank you.'

'Fortunate man.'

James Scobell lit a large cigar with care. He still acquired them from Cuba and thought that no sin, it was one of the perks of his dangerous trade. He smoked a good many

3

and moreover inhaled them; he had a graveyard cough but had decided to die with it. He repeated the young man's formula quietly.

'If I can help you?'

'Perhaps you can.'

Scobell had never cared for this game, meeting it with a blunt directness. 'Then tell me,' he said.

Peter van Ruyden considered carefully. His profession had taught him a certain caution, but he could see that if he played it all flannel and English allusions James Scobell would decline to play it back. 'I've been burgled,' he said at last and waited.

'Your flat, I take it?'

'Yes, my flat.'

'And you've told the police, no doubt?'

'Of course.'

'Much taken?'

'Quite a bit, I'm afraid.'

'Valuables? Silver? That sort of thing?' James Scobell inspected van Ruyden coolly. The clothes and the manner said valuables clearly—pictures, old silver, antiques, the lot. The van Ruydens were very rich indeed, old wealth of the indestructible kind. Wherever he lived he'd be living in style, not on his pay but what grandfather gave him. James Scobell was not a socialist but he hadn't much time for his country's van Ruydens. 'I'm sorry,' he said though he didn't sound it. He added as an afterthought, trying to keep his voice impersonal:

'Don't you have some sort of safe?'

'I do. And I use it.'

'So you lock your best things up in it?' He seemed more sensible than Scobell had supposed. 'So they blew your safe and took your stuff——'

'They didn't take any stuff at all.' Van Ruyden dis-

4

liked the word and showed it. 'Though there were one or two objects well worth taking.'

'What did they take, then?'

'They took some money.'

'A lot of it?'

'Fifty thousand pounds.'

James Scobell's heavy face showed no hint of surprise but privately he was badly shaken.... Fifty thousand English pounds. It was chicken feed to any van Ruyden, but if Scobell's suspicion was even half right the fact that it had been held in cash implied something was very near the boil, some action which James Scobell mistrusted.

Which meant that it might also be dangerous, embarrassing to all well-conducted Intelligence.

Van Ruyden was silent and Scobell reflected. The organization which he worked for himself was one which allowed of two opinions. Some people thanked their God it existed and to others it was a political menace, it had too much power, it was almost autonomous. James Scobell himself took the middle view. His organization made dreadful mistakes but it also had resounding successes. If the mistakes were egregious they were also inevitable since nothing born of woman was perfect. In the alarming world which existed today the men Scobell worked for had a necessary place, and if sometimes they used their power unwisely it was tempered by an essential limit. His seniors only played with the possible which a man like van Ruyden might misread disastrously.

Scobell repeated the scaring words quietly. 'Fifty thousand pounds,' he said. 'And I think you said you've told the police.'

'I did because I felt I must.'

James Scobell was relieved—that at least was orthodox. 'What did the police say?' he asked at length.

'The police were very helpful indeed. They did the routine checks and then came back, and a charming Inspector explained the position. There hadn't been any fingerprints but it appears there is only a handful of men who can blow a safe as neatly as that. My porcelain wasn't even cracked.'

... God damn your bloody rich man's porcelain.

'And so?' Scobell said.

'So it seems it's a simple elimination. Of this handful of men who could do the job four or five are safely in various prisons, and another three or four have alibis. Either they were out of the country or they could prove they were sitting quietly at home. Which leaves one man and the police know his name. It's a question of collecting evidence.'

'Quite a big question with that sort of operator.'

'The English police struck me as knowing their business.'

Yes, Scobell thought, no doubt they had. British Inspectors had mostly good manners and Peter van Ruyden would notice that. What else they were he would hardly care.

'And nothing was taken besides this money? How did the police account for that? Did they think there had been a previous tip-off about the money you happened to have in your safe?'

'They considered that very unlikely indeed but they thought it was a well-planned job in an area which they described as prosperous. The thief came prepared to blow a safe, so presumably he was expecting to find one. If he hadn't he might have stripped the apartment, but when he found he had fifty thousand in cash there wasn't much point in doing that.'

'Even if they get this man you'll never see your money back.'

Van Ruyden drew a deliberate breath; he didn't like it

6

but he must say it some time. 'It isn't the loss of the money which worries me.'

'There was something else taken?'

'I'm afraid there was.'

Scobell, who'd been losing interest, tautened. He had guessed that van Ruyden had not approached him merely for help in recovering money. The real reason was at last emerging.

'Something else?' he repeated.

'A document.'

'So?'

Scobell now wanted more time to think. It wouldn't be an official paper improperly taken home to study. This elegant wasn't as callow as that. He was a genuine First Secretary, properly trained, not a man from an East European embassy which used agents with diplomatic cover and where someone who might be cook or chauffeur could in a crisis give his ambassador orders. Scobell's country had more than its share of agents but that wasn't the way it normally used them. In the pinches it did but the pinch must be serious, and at the moment there was no such thing. James Scobell took a drag on his Cuban cigar; he coughed but controlled it; he said when he had his bronchial breath back:

'It might save time if we had this straight. You know what I do or you wouldn't be here, and I know you're a perfectly genuine diplomat, not an agent with diplomatic front. But I also know of some very odd cases where an amateur has succumbed to temptation.'

'You're well informed,' van Ruyden said.

It was a mistake to make his voice so acid. Scobell was an easy-going man but if there was one thing he loathed it was upper-crust patronage.

7

'I don't think I'm very well informed but I work for a competent organization.'

'I beg your pardon,' van Ruyden said stiffly.

'This document, then. What sort of document?'

'It was one which I was going to buy.'

'With the fifty thousand pounds?'

'Correct.'

'Where did it come from?'

'It came from a British Security Office. I was due to hand over the money next day.'

'Which Security Office?'

Peter van Ruyden told him reluctantly.

'What sort of document?'

'Must you know that?'

'I must if I'm going to help you.'

'Are you?'

'That depends on what you're prepared to tell me.'

Van Ruyden wasn't happy and showed it but he knew Scobell held his short hairs hard. He hesitated but said at last:

'It was a personal and high level estimate of how the Cabinet would react, individually, if China moved into North Vietnam.'

Scobell exploded. 'Christ Almighty!' His face went red but not in anger; he wanted badly to laugh but didn't like to.... The ignorance of these half-baked amateurs! Scobell carried no torch for his country's diplomats, their airs and graces often annoyed him, but he didn't believe they were all incompetent. There was an enormous establishment, it had to find work, and this sort of hypothetical guess was precisely what it was paid to make. Embassies were listening posts, legitimately employed to listen, to read newspapers, throw expensive parties, to meet everybody who mattered—assess them. This estimate (bloody silly word)

8

would be available at a few hours' notice if it wasn't already on Washington's files. And the Office which Peter van Ruyden had named was by no means the top of British Security. Its nickname in Scobell's world was contemptuous for they were the artisans, the sweepers-up. They did the dirty work, the regrettable rough stuff. Their opinion on a possible Cabinet meeting was less reliable than a top grade journalist's.

This Report, since you had to call it something, was so much rude paper too thick to be useful but the fact that it existed terrifying. This diplomat had suborned an official and that road could lead almost anywhere.

'You didn't tell this to the police?' Scobell asked. With this extraordinary boy even that was possible.

'What do you take me for?'

'That I'm not saying.' The cigar had gone out and Scobell lit another. 'Then the situation seems clear enough.'

'Not to me.'

'You should think. Let's approach it as an official would, a bent but still British civil servant. One.' Scobell held up an index finger. 'One. The police know of the theft and have guessed the thief.' He held up another finger. 'Two. The man who gave you that Report knows you had it, and now he'll also know of the safe-blowing. He'll know that from reading his daily blatts, the sort where a diplomat robbed makes a paragraph. When, by the way, did he hand this thing over?'

'The day before the safe was blown.'

'Then he'll also be very frightened indeed.'

Van Ruyden was becoming impatient. 'Where does this lead us?'

'Please listen to me, I hadn't finished.' James Scobell's third finger rose majestically. 'This contact of yours must

9

be high on his ladder so naturally he'll have police connections. Perfectly normal and perfectly proper.'

'And so?'

'So your contact will use his discreet connections, very possibly hinting at political overtones. Naturally he won't say what they are but the police wouldn't think that at all unusual. They'll play ball with a senior man in Security.'

'What sort of ball?'

'I'd have thought that obvious. They'll tell him the name of the man they suspect, when your contact will be obliged to look after him. He'll be obliged because he's in very grave danger.'

Van Ruyden was silent, taking it in. 'You really think that?' he asked at last. 'You'd do that yourself if the heat was on you?'

'What else could I do? Not that it's a meaningful question.' Scobell stared at van Ruyden, his temper cracking. 'I don't sell Reports to amateur agents, and even if I'd considered it I'd be careful about the prospective buyer.'

'I find that offensive.'

'I'm afraid it's a fact.'

Van Ruyden rose, then sat down again slowly. He was furious but he needed this man. 'I came for advice.'

'Advice costs nothing, I give it freely. There's no need at this moment for overt action and certainly none for action by me. Give the British themselves a chance— they may take it. Give them a week and if nothing happens we might have to look at this again.'

'Is that your advice professionally?'

'Yes.'

'I don't conceal you disappoint me.'

'Then I don't conceal you scare me stiff.'

'Good day,' van Ruyden said.

'Good day. And try to relax, it helps in judgement.'

When van Ruyden had gone Scobell went to a cupboard. He took out a bottle of whisky, half full, and methodically began to lower it. For an appalling thought had struck him brutally. As Intelligence that Report was valueless.

Suppose the van Ruydens knew it too.

2

Jack Shay was also a worried man though the reason was entirely different. Uneasiness would have better described a state of mind which seldom troubled him, for although he was a successful criminal and therefore exposed to the risks of his trade his success had been built upon caution and planning; he wasn't like other thieves he knew who would do a big job on a Friday night, then go after a couple of hundred on Sunday; he assessed the odds and played them scrupulously, turning down work which he thought too risky and always work which struck him as flashy. 'Flashy' meant simply catching the news, or rather the news in respectable newspapers. He had done some time but not a great deal. It worked out around twenty thousand pounds for every year in stir he'd done. Shay thought that a very fair business return and he considered himself a business-man.

It was an image he liked to cultivate—good suit, hand-some shoes and a very quiet tie, the rising executive, thirty-six. He had a house in a respectable suburb, a wife who accepted his trade without fuss, a solid and unpretentious car. He also had what top criminals must, a protector to mind the business end. The good ones were rather hard to come by since they had to be men from a different world, men who if the police suspected would be very hard indeed to nail. Paul Martiny was the best of these but he wouldn't accept you simply for money; he had to sympathize, to like you personally. Shay was sure that Paul Martiny liked him and he suspected that he liked his wife. Well, Judie could look after herself.

As Paul Martiny looked after Shay. Did the police put the heat on, was an absence advisable? Ten thousand pounds would appear in Mexico. Martiny knew how to work such things and he had a huge contempt for exchange control. He was shrewd at investing money too, Shay's savings had comfortably beaten inflation. Shay smiled his polite, faintly acid smile. Paul Martiny wasn't a Master Mind, something which after headline crimes the Press would insist had planned the whole thing: on the contrary he didn't want to know, would have silenced you if you'd tried to tell him. And he wasn't a fence, that was far too risky; he would handle your money and occasionally things, but only if he knew a safe market. Jewellery, for instance—he had that taped. Jewellery could be broken up easily and provided you were prepared to wait a good stone could be cut again and sold safely. His advice, moreover, was always sound. He was a man from a very different world but he understood how that world would think and when you made a mistake he could often help you.

That sealed envelope Shay had taken, for instance. He regretted that now, he had acted on impulse, but blowing a safe was hardly the moment for examining carefully double-sealed envelopes. He had swept it up with the bundles of notes since for all he knew it had held more money. He was certain that it didn't now, it was solid sheets of quarto paper and by the look of it must be something official. Jack Shay had decided not to open it. Anything smelling official alarmed him.

13

So he'd acted on impulse in taking the envelope but the police had been right about everything else. Shay had planned it as he always did, taking his time and weighing the chances. The information he'd needed he'd quietly bought, that van Ruyden was a diplomatist and the son of a very rich man indeed. He also had a collection of porcelain, though as Martiny wouldn't have looked at porcelain Jack Shay had never considered stealing it. But it was evidence that van Ruyden was rich as was the fact that he owned a modern safe.

Jack Shay had blown it and almost collapsed.... Fifty thousand pounds in tenners! In moments of extremest optimism he had thought of maybe five at most, but this was the sort of sensational sum which you got from the flash crimes he wouldn't go with. It was excusable that he hadn't thought deeply. He had cleaned out the safe and gone straight to Paul Martiny.

Who as usual had been coolly practical. 'You are about,' he had said, 'to change your class, to join a very select one indeed.'

'I don't want to change my class a bit.'

'You already have, you can't escape it. You are now a very rare bird indeed, the criminal who has really made it and can afford to retire in the odour of sanctity. Let me see.' Paul Martiny had reflected silently. 'You own your own house and that flat in Cyprus which together must be worth fifteen thousand. Your investments, when I last looked at them, were worth around another fifty, so with that and what you've just acquired you own two places and a hundred thousand. Invested in good industrial loans that's something like ten thousand a year. You could live on that very comfortably.'

'I mean to.'

14

'That's extremely wise. I'm sure your wife would approve of that.'

'You've asked her, then?'

'Of course I haven't. But I know she's a very sensible woman.'

... And I really believe that's all he knows yet. No doubt if I ever went back to stir ...

'And that envelope?' Jack Shay had asked.

'That's simply an embarrassment since you're sure that it doesn't contain more money.' Paul Martiny looked at Jack Shay hard. 'I can't think why you ever took it.'

'Nor can I now I come to think of it but at the moment I hadn't much time for thinking.'

'At least you haven't opened it.'

'No.'

'I think that was very wise again.'

'What'll you do with it?'

'Hold it for a bit while I think. Perhaps there's some way to return it. I'd like to.'

'You won't open it either?'

'Emphatically no.' Unexpectedly Martiny's voice had an edge. 'In many ways I'm an old-fashioned man—if I wasn't I wouldn't be very much use to you. Van Ruyden is a diplomatist and this envelope could be something secret. State secrets are something I've never dealt it. Nor do I wish to start now. That's final.'

'I wasn't considering blackmail, you know.'

'If you had been I wouldn't have looked at it. Now how do you want this money invested?'

'As you said, in high yielders.'

'You'll lose out on the inflation, of course.'

'We haven't any children.'

'I'm sorry.' Paul Martiny thought again. 'There's just

one thing—you mustn't be greedy. Don't go out on some silly job for the extra.'

'I'm honestly not a greedy man and Judie isn't a greedy woman.'

And now this successful criminal, a man with a hundred thousand pounds, was going out on a job which he didn't need. He hadn't chosen to do it; he'd simply been forced to.

Perhaps he should have foreseen what was coming but when you were young you didn't think much. At that moment he had been far from successful, just one of a thousand unthinking tearaways. He'd come up from the country and found himself work but he'd also found wild and lawless friends, and after the almost routine stupidities inevitably he had done his Borstal. This had taught him much that it wasn't designed to and he had a solid advantage the others had not. He'd been apprenticed to a famous locksmith, a firm with an international name.

They had dropped him at once at the first hint of trouble but they hadn't been able to take back his knowledge and he began to build on that methodically. An aunt had left him five hundred pounds and he used it to increase his skills. He went to a Technical College and learnt; he learnt about explosives and metals. Borstal had done what it hadn't intended and he began to climb his own ladder fast; he went to prison but not for long and all the time he was learning steadily.

He drank very little but used his local and one evening a stranger bought him a beer. They met again and then a third time, and on the fourth the man asked him back to his flat. And there Shay had been offered his first big job. The man had been very frank indeed, though to this day Jack Shay didn't know his real name. He had explained that he was employed by Security—Shay wouldn't expect him to say which part of it. They had a job to do on a trouble-

16

some foreigner, a spy who could be more than dangerous. Naturally they would co-operate, giving Shay all the information they had, but they didn't dare risk a man of their own even if they'd had the right one.

The fee would be ten thousand pounds.

At that time it had sounded a fortune to Shay and the information they'd shown had reassured him. Whatever else these people were they were thorough and careful, they knew what was needed.

Jack Shay did the job and drew his money. He didn't blow it but took it at once to Martiny. Ten thousand would interest even Paul Martiny whom he'd already decided he'd take his first stake to.

Eighteen months later the ten was fifteen. Shay had met Judie O'Neill and had married her.

And now he was thinking he should have foreseen it, that if he worked for these people they'd hold him for ever. But that had been ten years ago and he'd never heard another word.

Until the evening when the stranger called, driving up to the Shays' suburban home and leaving a noisy sports car outside it.

'Wife out?' he had asked as Shay answered the ring.

'If it's vacuum cleaners——'

'It isn't that, it's a man called Steiner. I believe you'll remember Ernest Steiner. He's the man you did some years ago.'

'If you're a Jack I'll see your warrant.' Shay had learnt all the rules and how to use them.

'I'm not the police and I don't have a warrant card. But I know your fee was ten thousand pounds and if you're sensible you'll realize what *that* means. May I come in?'

'If you bloody must,' Jack Shay had said. He didn't

often swear these days but when the heat was on he sometimes reverted.

The young man came in and sat down at once, not waiting for Shay's invitation to do so. He had bright red hair
and a hat with a feather which he carefully put on the
floor by his chair. Shay thought it a rather horrible hat but
the young man was clearly attached to it. He crossed his
legs and stared without speaking, trying to build up a
credible tension. Jack Shay had a sudden and sharp impression that this young man watched a good deal of telly.
When he'd completed his stare he said:

'We've got another job for you.'

'I don't want another job from you. I don't want another job from anyone.'

'I was afraid you might say that.'

'Then why come?'

'I came to persuade you.'

'You won't.'

'We can.'

Jack Shay was accustomed to thinking fast and had decided at once that this would be blackmail. What the lever
would be he couldn't yet tell, he'd have to bear with this
nasty young man and listen. But he didn't believe he would
talk to the police. That job had been ten years ago and in
any case this young man's masters had been just as much
involved as he had. If they opened their mouths then so
could he. It wouldn't matter that he had no proof, they'd
be scared of even a hint of involvement.

But the young man was playing his cards by the book
and the book said you kept the real high ones till last.
'It's a drug job,' he said.

'I never touch them.' Jack Shay was contemptuous, he
hated all drug traffics. This detestable man hadn't done his
homework. For a moment Shay felt almost confident.

18

It passed at once as the young man said: 'I know you don't.'

'Then why try to lean on me?'

'I'm asking for your co-operation.' He uncrossed his legs. 'Would you care to hear?'

'I can't throw you out, you're stronger than I am.'

The red-head looked absurdly flattered, relaxing the manner he'd learnt from the telly. 'Then there's far too much drug-pushing going on—at least we're both agreed on that—and some of it's of a very odd kind. This particular bit is done by an Indian and this Indian has official standing.'

Shay was interested rather than frightened now. He'd read cases of diplomats smuggling drugs but as far as he knew they'd been South Americans. That an Indian should be doing it too was something which offended him. They were a tiresomely self-righteous people who at the drop of a hat read you moral lectures, but that didn't stop them seizing territory nor now, apparently, dealing in drugs.

'And you'll realize,' the red-head young man was saying, 'that it's all as safe as the Bank of England. There are good reasons why the police won't touch it. There's still something called the Commonwealth and our relations with Mother India are tricky enough as it is already. Doing a diplomat for drugs would in any case mean a major rumpus, so you'll understand there's been heavy pressure to handle it in another way. But equally if the police can't bust him nor could this Indian go to the police. If anything went wrong, I mean. Not that it will—we know all about you. And the fee will be twenty thousand this time.'

It was the first real mistake which the visitor made since for an instant Jack Shay had been almost tempted. He was a thief but a man with a social conscience, heartily loath-

19

ing all dealing in drugs, and that a diplomatist should be deep in this evil, a man with a special position and privileges, was something which he found hard to take. But the mention of money had promptly steadied him. Paul Martiny had warned him straitly that the one thing he mustn't be was greedy and in any case Jack Shay judged his risks. There'd been a time when twenty thousand pounds would have tempted him very severely indeed but twenty thousand more on the hundred he had didn't strike him as a sound proposition. 'No,' he said sharply, 'no, I won't do it.'

The young man resumed his telly manner. 'That's really very unfortunate.'

'Why?'

'We could make things very awkward.'

'How?'

'There's that shop of your wife's.'

'It isn't bent.'

'I know it isn't but that's the point.'

The young man waited and Jack Shay thought. Judie had bought a failing boutique from a young woman who'd come into too much money and had looked on a trendy boutique as a hobby. When she'd lost enough she had sold to Judie, and Judie with her Ulster shrewdness had seen that what the area needed wasn't more boutiques—there were plenty already—but a discreet and rather expensive shop to appeal to the women of solid means, the custom which otherwise went to London. She had thrown out all the trendy rubbish and stocked up with what was quietly good. She loved the work and was making it pay.

And this unpleasant young man could break all that since in the rag trade the image was all important. A whisper here and a whisper there ... Jack Shay could think of parts of London where the customers might have thought it smart that their dressmaker was the wife of a criminal.

20

But not in this suburb. Certainly not. Not the ladies who bought from Judie Shay.

Shay looked at this hard young man with hatred. He would do it too, he was that sort of man.

Jack Shay was very fond of his wife, he admired her and he valued her virtues. Loyalty was an unmodish word but she had given it without reservation. He never told her about his jobs, one didn't, but when something was in the wind she knew it, and though she would tense she never nagged him. Stealing was his profession. So be it.

And now she had started this shop and enjoyed it. It was her baby and she looked ten years younger. He couldn't take that away from her especially as she hadn't another. 'What a bastard you are,' he said at last, but behind the abuse he was thinking hard.

But he hadn't decided yet; he was careful. If it were possible to avoid doing so then he wouldn't let Judie down with a bump, but also he wouldn't accept a risk which ran against all the sensible odds. He heard himself saying: 'Where is this job?'

'A couple of miles from here. House like this one.'

'A safe, of course?'

'Of course there is. If there weren't we shouldn't be coming to you. There are hundreds of break-and-enter men.'

'What gen have you got to give me?'

'Plenty. The safe is a rotten old foreign thing.'

'Make and year?'

He was told.

Jack Shay was impressed: it was worth going on. 'Household arrangement?' he asked at length.

The red-head passed over a typewritten paper. 'The address is on that and what really matters. On Tuesday this Indian and his wife will be out. Some diplomatic dinner-do.

They've five children but they'll be parked with friends. Casing the joint is up to you.'

'These drugs are in the safe?'

'They are. Heroin in an attaché case. This man has a diplomatic visa, and though he was something more than suspect for the reasons I gave you they didn't bounce him. It's quite a big attaché case. A quarter of a million pounds' worth of hell.'

'You just want the case?'

'Not another thing. If possible we should like it unopened. There's some legal point which I don't understand.'

And now Jack Shay had done his reconnaissance; he had broken in quietly and blown the safe. He had done it with contemptuous ease, for as the young man had told him the safe was old iron. It had struck him as being typically Indian, a quarter of a million pounds' worth of evil and a safe which a competent boy could have broken.

He took the case and shut the safe, looking around him with rising anger. He was tempted to smash the place up a bit, that might make it look like some local tearaway, but there wasn't a local tearaway who could blow a safe as he'd blown this one. Besides, there was nothing much worth smashing. This man was in the most beastly of trades but he didn't spend freely on creature comforts. Instead, Shay thought savagely, he just begat children. But he wouldn't be selling his own children heroin. It was other men's children who paid and were broken.

He had parked his car three streets away and as he came to it a man touched his shoulder. There was another behind him, alert and poised.

'We're police officers.' They showed their cards.

'A parking rap?' Shay knew it wasn't. He'd had a lookout who should have been back in the car. He had stolen it but that was routine. He always abandoned them quite

22

undamaged. He was a peterman not a man who smashed
motorcars.

'You're Jack Shay, I believe.'

To deny it was pointless.

'We'd like to see what you've got in that case.'

'Maybe you would.' Shay knew this game.

'Very well, at the station.'

The policeman produced a radio and Shay listened to the
jargon silently. Within a minute there was a big black
police car.

'You want me to come to the station?'

'Yes.'

'If you mean to arrest me I won't resist it.'

The policeman smiled. 'I can see you're Jack Shay. All
right, if you want it that way. I arrest you.'

'Awkward if this case holds pyjamas.'

'Very awkward indeed but we're going to risk it.'

At the station there was a senior officer, uniformed and
grim but careful.

'I'd be grateful to know what's inside that case.'

'Meaning you'll find the get-out easier if I open it and
there's nothing to interest you.'

The Inspector didn't answer him.

'Suppose I said that I didn't know. Suppose I just said
that I hadn't a key.'

'Key or no key you could open it blindfold.'

'A judge wouldn't like that remark a bit.'

The Inspector who'd had his promotion delayed for
ignoring the book as a station sergeant changed his manner
to what he hoped was sweet reason. 'Then why don't you
simply *tell* us what's in it. It's just possible we might believe you.'

'I'm under arrest—I saw to that. But I haven't yet been
charged or cautioned.'

23

The Inspector gave up, made a sign to a constable. They brought him keys and the third one fitted.

Inside was some cheap-looking Indian silver.

3

Paul Martiny had been born in a world whose advantages he gladly accepted but whose values he considered nonsense. He was what was still called a country gentleman since they lived in the country and were deemed to be gentle, and the criminals whose affairs he managed assumed that he did it for lack of money. The landed class had been properly clobbered, and if one of them needed an outside income then the best of British luck to him. This was the general opinion. Mistakenly. Paul Martiny owned three thousand acres. All were in hand and all were farmed excellently. He'd had the capital for modernization and the land paid a decent return on its value. As for the huge and pretentious house he had pulled it down without a pang. The place had been an Edwardian horror and no Preservation Order barred him. He'd built a good modern house and he lived in it comfortably, he and his placid conventional lady. So he didn't need money, he needed escape, relief from a world which would otherwise strangle him. Some men of his kind could find it in sport and others in simple if squalid venery. Paul Martiny was too clever for either; he found his release in helping criminals.

And helping was a word of precision since that was also what he openly did. He had sat on his County Council for years and once he'd been a Deputy Lieutenant, but what he was known for was work with ex-prisoners; he sweated on earnest and pompous committees, concealing a patrician contempt for people he mostly considered wet. These penologists, for instance—stupid. (And what in hell did a penologist *do*?) He'd been horrified when they'd trapped him on telly and the panel had talked for half an hour, not one of them daring to use the word punishment. Paul Martiny wasn't an intellectual, and a criminal who did too much time was a criminal who had failed at his job. There was a price for that as there was for all failure.

But this tedious work was perfect cover for it gave him his contacts and a place in their world. What this brought him prevented him going mad, but this was Martiny's private business.

He was drinking a morning gin in his club, conscious that another member was trying to work up the courage to speak to him. He knew this man by name and repute but nobody had introduced them and there was a tradition in this club of his that you waited until somebody did so. Martiny didn't consider this stuffy: it was more civilized than that other place where you couldn't read a paper at lunch and the members talked their heads off incessantly. Here you could be social enough if company was what you wanted but equally you could quietly hole up and no boring old judge told you endless stories. Paul Martiny sipped his gin and waited, and the other man rose from the bench and came over.

'I hope I'm not intruding.'

'Of course not. I'm Paul Martiny and I know your name.'

It was more than politeness, he did know the name. This barrister was becoming eminent, a strong Junior at the criminal bar, and he'd defended Martiny's friend, Jack Shay. Paul Martiny despised all lawyers but this one had

26

put up a fine defence. His case hadn't had a leg to stand on but he'd done what he could and had done it well. Martiny said:

'Will you have a drink?'

'That's very kind. A whisky, please.'

Whisky at lunch-time Martiny thought barbarous but he ordered a large one—no ice and water. The lawyer said:

'Do you mind if I talk? I defended a man called Jack Shay and you know him.'

Paul Martiny didn't attempt to duck since his cover made any such action pointless. 'I know you did and I watched you do it. As you say, I've an interest in Shay, an old one. When he came out of jail some years ago we tried to keep him on the straight and narrow, and when he slipped again he sent for me and asked me to keep an eye on his wife.'

A woman, Paul Martiny was thinking, whom I'd have certainly kept an eye on anyway.

'The work you do must have disappointments.'

'If it didn't I wouldn't find it rewarding.' He had put on his dogooder's face to say it. It was the side of this work which he found the hardest, the occasional need to look earnestly righteous.

'Can I talk to you freely?'

'I hope you can.'

The bar wasn't crowded but without a word spoken they had taken their drinks to the furthest corner where the barman couldn't hear their talk. The barrister stared at his whisky hard, then he said on a note of strain: 'I'm troubled.'

'The Shay case? Yes, I agree it's troubling. It's such waste of a potentially useful man.' It was the orthodox thing to say so he said it. 'But if you don't mind a layman saying so I thought that you handled it very well.'

'It isn't that which bothers me.'

'No?'

The barrister drank some whisky slowly. Paul Martiny understood him perfectly. He was struggling with a good lawyer's reticence which in turn fought the human desire to talk. He finished the whisky and bought another, bringing a second gin for Martiny. As he sat down he made up his mind. 'The whole case stank to heaven,' he said.

'You're not suggesting it was a put-up job?'

'No, I'm not saying that though my lay client did. He told me an extraordinary story, and frankly I didn't believe a word. It was a tale about some work he'd once done for some Security people he didn't name and who'd used it to blackmail him ten years later. So they'd forced him to do that job in Surbiton but told him that he was after heroin. There wasn't an iota of evidence and anyway I didn't believe it.'

Martiny said: 'And nor do I.'

More accurately he hadn't decided. He didn't believe this preposterous story which was the sort of yarn criminals often told you, but he'd heard stranger ones and twice they'd had substance. He had seen Jack Shay since he'd been taken to prison and Shay had said nothing to him of this. But then how could he? Unlike a visit from an accredited lawyer Paul Martiny's had not been privileged. Shay had asked him to look after his wife. He hadn't said anything else whatever.

Paul Martiny swirled the gin in his glass. 'If you don't believe this incredible story I don't follow why the case should worry you.'

'It was too open-and-shut, too slick, too smooth.'

'If you mean that someone had grassed that's obvious, but it doesn't disturb my private conscience. The police have their sources of information. If they hadn't we couldn't sleep safe in our beds.'

28

'But who grassed?'

'I don't know.'

'I can tell you who didn't—it wasn't his look-out. Shay's always been very careful indeed. He picked the man up just an hour before, then the pair of them stole a car and went off. The look-out never had previous knowledge.'

'Then a second thief who also knew?'

'I think not. Shay keeps himself to himself. That's his record.'

'I agree that there's something a little odd.'

'I'm damned sure that there's something more than odd.'

Paul Martiny was watching the lawyer. For the moment he had forgotten his trade, he was simply a very unhappy citizen. 'It smells,' he said again.

'Of what?'

But the lawyer wasn't quite ready to answer. 'Well, look at the way the police behaved.'

'Police brutality? Shay didn't complain of it.'

'Quite to the contrary—smooth as oil. And the things they did to make sure of Shay! They picked up the look-out outside the house, a man whom they knew had a bit of form, but they didn't attempt to protect the property, they waited till Shay came out before acting.' Something of his court manner came back to him. 'I put it to you that they *knew* it was Shay; they *knew* he was going to blow a safe but they didn't attempt to prevent his doing so. They wanted a cast-iron case. They got it.'

'I'm up to the neck in ex-prisoners' aid but I'm not the sort which traduces the police. If what you say is right it was tough, but being a policeman is pretty tough work.'

'You mustn't suppose that I'm passing judgement. All that interests me is the evidence.'

'But evidence of what?'

'Foreknowledge.'

Martiny said: 'And of course where it came from.'

'Are you interested too?'

'Indeed I am.'

'Then let's start from the beginning again. I told you I didn't believe Shay's story, but suppose it was even a quarter true, suppose you just took it at five per cent.'

'But which five per cent are you going to take?'

The barrister drank up his whisky slowly, then said in a voice which was almost apology: 'Those Security people Shay didn't name. *The people who might have tipped off the police.*'

'But you can't just accept that in isolation. If the rest of the story were true it makes nonsense. They'd be jailing a man who was doing a job for them.'

'Do you ever read spy stories?'

Martiny smiled. 'If you mean have I heard of blown agents I have. But I don't believe Jack Shay was an agent.'

'Nor do I come to that and that's my trouble. And I'm in court this afternoon—Shay's appeal.'

'I knew he was appealing.'

'In effect on the sentence though there isn't much hope.'

'I think I'll come down and see what happens.'

'Court of Appeal in the Criminal Division, what used to be the old C.C.A. Three o'clock and they mostly run to time.'

'I'd like to see the Court of Appeal.'

It had sounded sufficiently cool and casual but to Martiny it would mean a real effort. A court of law made him physically ill, even the local magistrates' bench which he'd steadfastly refused to sit on. It racked his nerves, it stirred his bile. He wasn't consciously an iconoclast, and if the national game was controlled by backwoodsmen, if senior churchmen were clearly senile, he didn't burn up to pull them down. But it reinforced his natural instinct that this

30

establishment he'd been born into was very near its final
end. There were people who wore their hair too long, who
marched in processions and strummed guitars, but Martiny
thought that wholly pointless. It did nothing but astonish
the bourgeois, which was something which only satisfied
children, whereas if you'd been born an insider you could
show your contempt without foolish posing. It was even,
in its compulsive thrust, a pleasure to do just that. He took
it. He took it by managing Shay and three others, and if
contempt showed any sign of flagging a court of law would
always revive it. You paid for attendance with real disgust
but you left in a towering rage, hate confirmed.

Martiny took a taxi to Fleet Street and walked through
the pseudo-gothic hall; he went up the stairs and turned
right, then left. The doorman had told him where to find it.
He went in and sat down and his stomach tightened.

It was worse than he had let himself fear, the dim light
and the long book-lined walls, the air of ancient men preserved, the calculated mummery. On the benches in front
were Counsel whispering, and behind them were students,
a handful of foreigners and the nondescript men who
haunted courts. Presently they brought in Shay. He didn't
stare round the court but sat down listlessly. Martiny
looked at his watch: it was five to three. Their Lordships
would have taken their luncheons and very possibly a quiet
nap as well.

When the judges came in on the dais all stood up. The
three men bowed and they all sat down again. Paul Martiny
found himself astonished, astonished at his twinge of
pity.... These apart old men, so wise, so foolish. Incorrupt-
ible no doubt, but absurd. They weren't wearing scarlet but
gowns and bob wigs, and of the three of them only one
came near fitting. The man's in the middle was much too
small, it looked as though he had hired it too hastily.

31

Perhaps he thought it didn't matter: to Paul Martiny it mattered bitterly. If you played this game you should play it decently An ill-dressed charade came too close to arrogance.

The man in the middle nodded downwards and Martiny's fellow-clubman stood up, beginning at once on the question of sentence. Martiny smiled wryly—this wasn't full dress. Some flavour of the farce would be lost, no nice legal points to maul and chew over, no private esoteric game of poker where the stakes were paid by the man in the dock. Instead it was a straight plea for pity.

But he conceded that this barrister was doing his job very well indeed. His manner was precisely right. The four of them were all boys together but of course he was the junior boy.... Your Lordships may feel, Your Lordships may very well consider. They might consider, for instance, the facts before them. Shay had a record but not a long one and for four years there had been nothing against him. It was lamentable that he'd fallen again but at least the unfortunate man had tried. Was a sentence of eight years appropriate, was it really in the man's own interest?

The barrister's manner subtly changed for now he was on delicate ground. The trial judge had been a pompous one and his fellows in this court would know it; he had read Shay a long and tedious lecture, talking about the public weal, and this Lord Justice of Appeal and his brethren much preferred it when it was kept impersonal. It wouldn't displease these learned men to show their ageing but still formidable teeth against a man whom the barrister knew they thought shaky. But that was the last thing he dared to say. To knock a trial judge on a point of law was acceptable since within the rules, but even a hint he was old and incompetent, a survival from another age, and at once they'd close the ranks against you. Just the same he

32

was putting it over beautifully. Not a word which could be pinned down as criticism but the three men on the dais were getting the message. Counsel sat down after just ten minutes. It had neither been too long nor too short.

The judges began to chat together and one of them polished his spectacles briskly. It wasn't possible to guess from their manner which way these three old crows would fly. The two on the outside had left their seats, but after their chat they went back to them stiffly. The man in the middle began to speak.

... They had given most careful consideration and they hadn't been left entirely unmoved by an extremely able presentation. (They always said that, Martiny knew, even when the man had been terrible. It was part of this frightening timeless game.) So they hadn't been quite unmoved by the plea but they still couldn't see a valid reason for disturbing what seemed a justified sentence.

Paul Martiny looked at Jack Shay in the dock. For the first time he seemed aware of his presence. He raised his hand in a half salute but Shay gave him a look of black despair.

Martiny went back to his flat to think, knowing a major decision hung over him. Like the lawyer he hadn't believed Shay's story but he did believe that Shay had been shopped since the evidence had pointed that way and there wasn't a better explanation. It had been true that Shay mostly worked alone but on the facts the police must have had foreknowledge, so the question was how they had come by it, more precisely who had given it and behind the giving the giver's motive. But Martiny knew something the barrister hadn't. Shay had just robbed a diplomat of an unexpectedly large sum of money, but apart from the money he'd also taken a document. The envelope was here, still unopened, and it might, it just

33

might, be the key to the puzzle. It could also be a hot potato.

It might be a very hot one indeed, and Martiny, who preferred things cool, was reluctant to commit himself. The decision would be irreversible since if he opened that paper he'd always *know*. Managing thieves' affairs was one thing, it satisfied a sardonic humour, but he wasn't prepared to dive right in. He caused money which he knew was stolen to reappear in other countries; he advised criminals how to invest their loot; he arranged discreet exiles when those became necessary and occasionally he would handle stones though only when he knew a safe market. But he'd always kept aloof from the detail, the murderous pressures of criminals' lives. He wasn't a romantic man and he didn't hold the modish view that society was the authentic criminal, not the people who happened to break its laws. The criminal world and the way it lived had no attractions for Paul Martiny, esquire. In a sense he was simply using them, his escape from a way of life which bored him and which he happened to think was mostly rotten. It was better than shooting tigers, more satisfying. Any damned fool could shoot an animal but you needed a brain to manage criminals. That was Martiny's cross, he was clever, and the world he'd been born in suspected brains. But if you used a man you had obligations, and though criminals in the mass were distasteful Martiny had rather liked Jack Shay.

And he something more than liked his wife.

He made himself tea and picked up a novel; he'd let his decision come quietly, naturally. Like many clever but not academic men he believed in unconscious cerebration.

Presently he began to feel hungry and he boiled himself a couple of eggs. He had missed his lunch which he often did and in London he lived very simply indeed, just the one big room with a kitchenette. When he'd taken it his wife hadn't commented but he knew that she had assumed the worst. She would, he thought, she couldn't have helped it.

He looked at her framed photograph, raising a hand in ironical greeting. She wasn't a bad old butty really, and in her placid way she had kept her looks. It was simply that she was stiflingly conventional. Of course she had never had much chance—that preposterous old father of hers and that woman he'd married somewhere in Germany. She'd been some sort of obscure German noblewoman and for Martiny's taste, which was solidly English, much more noble than a real lady need be. They had brought up their daughter like a Victorian miss. She had all of that age's negative virtues but her parents had been too high on the ladder to pass her the era's saving gusto, its drive and its unashamed competitiveness. Paul Martiny didn't dislike his wife, it was simply that she sapped his vitality. She could wither him like a late spring frost, but quite innocent of intention to do so.

So naturally she had assumed the obvious, that her husband had a girl in London, except that she wouldn't have thought 'a girl', her mental phrase would be 'bit of nonsense'. And poor Matty would have been wrong again for he wasn't keeping a woman in London. Since she'd hinted in that way of hers that a man of forty slept in the dressing-room he hadn't been living as priests were supposed to, but nor was he wasting his time and substance on a woman who might make awkward demands. He wasn't a conceited man who believed that by snapping his fingers they'd come, but he was forty and he had kept his figure, he had crisp dark hair which he wore rather short, the parting a neat white weal on his scalp. He discharged, without trying, an unequivocal maleness, and he could

35

walk into an Alpino restaurant and a girl in a corner, alone, would smile. So he wasn't keeping a woman in London but nor was the divan bed a single.

He finished his eggs and washed up neatly. A woman came in to clean—that was all. When he needed a proper meal he went out and when he didn't he simply cooked for himself. Food wasn't a matter he cared about greatly and his waist was an elegant thirty-four.

And as he washed up he knew he'd decided. He was going to open that envelope. Now. It was a choice of evils. So be it, he'd made it.

He slit both envelopes and began to read quickly, whistling softly when he'd finished the pages. Unlike James Scobell who'd been bred in Intelligence this recital of Ministers' private leanings, of which way they would jump in a major crisis, didn't strike him as a load of nothing, something which any competent embassy would have sent to its masters years ago; he read it simply as a citizen, as a piece of what was clearly treason. This George Amyas who had signed was a traitor.

He had always believed the establishment rotten but he hadn't believed that its salaried pillars could be bought like this for alien money. They were bent every day but the bending was subtler; they were bought by promotion and honours, not cash. Was advice unwelcome? You quietly withdrew it. Six months later, maybe, you received your promotion.

But he would think about that later, not now. Now he had to think practically, quickly. For a practical mind had clicked at once. That story of Shay's had been basically true, though since Shay hadn't seen this outrageous paper he was probably still in the dark as to motive. But the rest fitted in like a well cut jigsaw.... Jack Shay had robbed a diplomat who'd been dealing in matters outside diplomacy and who'd suborned a man called Amyas to betray what no public servant should. Then this Amyas hears of the diplomat's burglary and he'd know that the diplomat held his paper, or at least that he had held it once. It was a guess when it had been handed over but the fact that Jack Shay had found fifty thousand, ready to pay but still unpaid, suggested very shortly before. In which case the diplomat might still have the paper, in which case the thief could have taken it too. So George Amyas is a frightened man, this Amyas has to cover up fast. He hasn't time to ask questions, he has to act.

The rest was at the best good guessing but in its ominous way it also fitted. This paper smelt of quite high Security and if that were right its contemptible author would have connections with the ordinary police. There was only a handful of petermen who could do a job with Shay's stamp of class, and if criminals co-operated naturally the establishments did so too. And if the smell of a Security background were right this Amyas would command resources which the police and the ordinary man did not. It was a fair assumption he'd used them ruthlessly; he had framed Jack Shay, he had got his man.

Paul Martiny sat up sharply, frowning. George Amyas had shopped Jack Shay but he hadn't yet recovered his paper. He couldn't possibly know of Paul Martiny's interest nor guess who now held his potential destruction, but he could guess just the same and would guess it wrong ... Judie Shay who was still in her house. Alone.

Martiny went to the telephone quickly, dialling a man whom he'd helped legitimately. He had found him a job when he'd come out of prison and the man had been grateful and anxious to show it. Moreover he was still going straight, which made him useful for Martiny's purpose.

37

'Paul Martiny here.'

'Good evening, squire.'

'Would you care to earn a few extra quid? I needn't say it's entirely straight.'

'A few extra quid are always handy.'

'You knew Jack Shay?'

'They gave him eight years and I thought it a cow.'

'I'm worried about his wife.'

'The law? You can never shake the bastards off.'

'No, not the law—you don't need to know. I want an eye kept on her house, that's all.' He gave the address. 'Can do?'

'Not properly. I've got this job you found me and I don't want to lose it.'

'I can run to thirty quid a day. With a couple of mates that's eight-hour shifts. Eight hours for a tenner and all tax free.'

'What do you want us to do?'

'Just watch. If there's anything or anybody you don't like the look of phone me at once. Here first but if it doesn't answer ring me in the country instead. You know the number. Reverse the charges.'

'Okay since it's you, sir.'

'Good night, then.'

'Right.'

4

He was packing next morning to return to the country when the bell rang and he opened the door. The caller removed his hat politely.

'May I come in?'

'Of course. Please do.'

The Chief Inspector came in and sat down solidly. He wore a good tweed suit and an ancient hat, stout shoes which were very carefully kept. He looked like a prosperous yeoman farmer which was precisely what he wished to look like. 'I was wondering if perhaps you could help us.'

'I will if I can.'

Paul Martiny meant it. The visit had in no way alarmed him for this Chief Inspector sat with him on a legitimate and occasionally useful committee, and in a world which was often airy-fairy a realistic policeman was a valuable ally. Martiny had sometimes asked himself if the police could suspect what he really did, that behind the cool front of public service was a man who managed criminals' money. He had decided that if they did have suspicions they'd be suspicions of a general kind. The police didn't believe in the Master Mind but they'd know that a successful criminal would need a man from a different world to help him, not in planning his crimes—he'd refuse to listen—but in handling the major proceeds, all the business of money, investments and transfers, where even the upper crust of criminals were as often as not simply babes in the wood. So maybe there was a handful of seniors with a list which they sometimes pulled out and wondered, and it wasn't quite inconceivable that Martiny was a name on that list. Equally there was no reason to think so. He had always been very careful indeed and in any case this Chief Inspector, a specialist in the traffic in gold, was hardly the man to have seen such a list, assuming that it even existed. So Martiny repeated: 'I'll help if I can.'

The Inspector said: 'It's Jack Shay. You know him.'

It was a statement of fact, entirely amiable, and in any event a denial was pointless. Martiny had seen Shay in prison and the Inspector would probably know of that. Martiny replied without hesitation.

'He knew I'd a pretty wide interest in prisoners and he asked me to go and see him. I did. He was worried about his wife but that's normal. I said I'd keep an eye on her.'

'You didn't ask why he was worried?'

'Of course not—how could I? It was an ordinary and routine visit. There was a screw around and you know the form. He didn't have his ears pinned back, he was looking out of the window hard, but there he was, not too close but *around*.'

'Yes, I know the form on that sort of visit.' The Inspector lit a short black pipe. In private he much preferred cigarettes but the pipe was a part of the image, a prop. 'I'd better lay them down,' he said.

'If you feel that you ought to by all means do so. Naturally I'm giving no undertaking.' Paul Martiny, too, knew the form very well.

'I wouldn't presume to ask for one.'

'Good.'

'So I have to accept the established facts and one of them looks pretty queer. I don't hide that the police had a tip-off on Shay and it's no business of mine to inquire where it came from. But Jack Shay was tried and duly sentenced for blowing an Indian diplomat's safe and stealing a load of indifferent silver. Now what do you make of that?'

'I don't.'

'I do, and what I make is unusual. Shay has always been very careful and thorough; he plans his jobs and on good information. Since all he got here was some Indian trash I'm obliged to believe that for once in a way the information he worked on was partly wrong.'

Martiny said quickly: *'Partly* wrong.'

'I wouldn't be here if all had been wrong.' The Inspector drew on his pipe with distaste. 'You know something of Jack Shay's world—how it works. The word goes around and it's often well founded. Such and such a factory draws its wages on a Thursday morning, or such and such a shop-keeper does the bulk of his trade on a Saturday morning but doesn't bank it till the following Monday. That's the background and it's often accurate. Here some of it was accurate but I suspect that the rest misled Jack Shay.' The pipe had gone out and he put it away. 'For there *is* another Indian diplomat whose safe would be very well worth doing. He smuggles out gold when he visits India and the profit on that is unbelievable.' The Inspector leant forward, suddenly sharp. 'Gold is very much my business and if Shay had happened to drop a hint——'

'He said nothing of this.' It was perfectly true. This Inspector was an intelligent man and if he'd put the pieces together wrongly he had done so on a credible theory. Paul Martiny had the authentic story but he didn't propose to pass it on. For one thing it wasn't his story to pass and for another it wasn't this policeman's pigeon.

'I was hoping Shay might have given a lead. We know all about this Indian, enough to put to a normal Department, but you know how the diplomats hang together. Unless we can prove it cut and dried the Foreign Office will stall and dither and we want him declared *non grata* —recalled. So we're looking for the source Shay acted on.'

'It's a hypothesis there even was one. If I had to I could make other guesses.'

'Better ones?'

'Not better ones, I concede you that. As I understand it you think Shay was after that gold, on information received through the usual net. That information, you tell me, was right enough, but unhappily they picked the wrong Indian. It's a defensible theory and maybe it's right but Jack Shay didn't even hint at it. He was worried about his wife—I told you.'

'When their men go inside they're terribly vulnerable. The jackals gather——'

'I know they do.'

'We try to help them if they come to us.'

'I know that too and so does Shay, but I also know the police are short-handed. I've been able to help a man or two and a few of them are actively grateful. Some are even trying to go straight again.'

'I wasn't asking,' the Chief Inspector said.

'I know you weren't, you're much too discreet.' The telephone rang and Martiny took it. There was the whine of a London voice, then silence. Martiny said: 'Hold' and turned to the other. 'This is a call from Judie Shay or rather from the man I put on her. There's been a visitor whom he doesn't know. He doesn't like the look of him and he's certain he isn't a plainclothes policeman.'

42

The Chief Inspector made an instant decision. 'Tell your man to do nothing rash but wait. You'll be coming at once and so will I. That is if I may and I think I should.'

'Delighted to have you,' Martiny said. For the second time he really meant it.

It was four months since van Ruyden had called on Scobell, months during which his own emotions had swung from a delighted relief that a means had been found to shut a man's mouth to reluctantly facing the ominous fact that he'd heard nothing about the Report itself. George Amyas hadn't contacted him and the situation was far too delicate to risk forcing the issue and earning a brush-off. He had finally gone to Scobell again though it hadn't been easy to make himself do it. He was saying now with a stiff formality:

'I've called again to offer my thanks. You advised me to give the British a chance; you implied that they'd act and they have indeed.'

Scobell had been doing some thinking himself and the results had been less than reassuring. His first thought had been of some amateur spying, for in his own, his extremely alarming country there would be men who would be prepared to back it. There was one in a south-western State who was supposed to maintain a private army. When communism came he'd fight it, defending civilization's last outpost. That was comic, a megalomaniac's dream, but van Ruyden had no need to work for one, not when he was Julius van Ruyden's grandson.... The enormous power of ancient wealth, amassed over generations, unshakeable. It stood behind major corporations, in the shadows for preference but always present, an establishment like no other on earth, known to exist but never tangible. Try to grasp it and there was nobody there,

43

just the railroads and steelworks and oil and land, all held firmly behind some legal screen. It was fashionable to discount all this, to say that a generation ago perhaps there had been this secret piracy, but not now, we've grown up, we're responsible now. James Scobell had good reason to know this was false. The methods and most of the men had changed, but not the objectives, they never would. Certainly not for old Julius van Ruyden, who'd care nothing for an abstract idea, nothing for theories of fighting communism. His enemy would be simply change, any change which could threaten established privilege.

'You say your friends have successfully acted?'

'I'm sure of it.'

'But how do you know?'

'It was conveyed to me rather prettily. When I came here before I think I mentioned that a charming Inspector explained the position. They hadn't found any fingerprints but it appeared there was an obvious suspect. You developed that yourself convincingly—how the police and my contact would find means to co-operate—and it seems to have happened exactly like that. My charming policeman has called again and I don't know how much he really knew. But what he said was enough to confirm your prophecy. Perhaps it was an accident but my Inspector even let drop a name. He explained that the police had been morally certain that my safe had been blown by a man called Shay, but they were sorry they were unlikely to nail him since a week or so later he'd been caught on another job red-handed.' Van Ruyden smiled but not with humour. 'In the light of what you said yourself I do not believe that was just coincidence.'

'If it wasn't it was mighty slick work.'

'You said the British could be efficient sometimes. So either this job was genuine and my contact found out and

44

tipped off the police, or else it was an organized frame-up.'

James Scobell could have wished that Peter van Ruyden would speak with a somewhat less evident relish but his conclusion he considered sound. The Security Office he'd named to Scobell was far from the top of British Security but in the world of the dirty work it did its reputation was one of extreme unscrupulousness. Scobell stared at Peter van Ruyden curiously. He thought him a typical east coast twit, over-educated and too clever by half, but he was also Julius van Ruyden's heir. There was a mystery here and Scobell disliked them, a threat which he couldn't pin down or define. All he knew from a lifetime's devoted work was that no menace was ever a jot less for the fact that you didn't know its nature.

But this boy had suborned an English official. That was dangerous enough to be going on with. And he was hardly the man to call again simply to express his thanks.

'So your friend fixed this Shay who blew your safe. Duly convicted, I take it?'

'Eight years. He lost on his appeal, what's more.'

'Eight sounds about right.'

'They ought to have shot him.'

James Scobell swallowed but didn't speak. Property, he was thinking—the rich. You could starve your dog or beat your baby but steal from the rich and they talked about bullets. He calmed himself though it cost an effort, watching van Ruyden again, more closely. A less careful man would have laid it down, knowing that with the James Scobells it paid to show your openers promptly. Scobell decided he'd have to help him; he had a shrewd idea of van Ruyden's worry.

'How long ago did they fix this thief?'

'It's about four months since they pulled him in. Then the trial and of course the appeal as well.'

45

'During which you haven't called here again.'

'You think I have been remiss? I apologize.'

'I don't think you've been remiss but you're stalling.'

'Please tell me on what.'

'Indeed I will.' Scobell blew cigar smoke hard at the ceiling. 'They've got your thief but not your Report.'

'How do you know?'

'If they had you'd have told me. Also it's the only reason you could bring yourself to come back to me.'

'You've worked it out,' van Ruyden said. He said it with relief but reluctance. It wasn't easy to give this calm man best.

'I assure you it wasn't difficult, but if you've decided that I'm not quite stupid do you mind if I ask the questions now?'

'That might be simpler.'

'Yes, it would.... Has anybody approached you yet?'

'What sort of approach?'

'From your contact, the man who signed that Report.'

Peter van Ruyden shook his head.

'From anyone else? For money? Blackmail?'

'No, not a thing.'

'That doesn't surprise me, Mr Shay is in jail. You can't do much damage from normal prison.'

'But when he comes out?'

'You won't be in England.'

'But the man who wrote that Report for me will.'

'Perfectly true—for your friend very dangerous.'

'Then why is he still dragging his feet? I mean about getting back that Report.'

'Because the immediate heat is off him. When your safeblower went to jail he bought time but that doesn't mean he'll do nothing for ever. Sooner or later this

46

Shay will come out and when he does he'll have a weapon. He'll have that damnfool Report of yours. Your friend can't afford that, he daren't afford it.'

'And so,' van Ruyden asked, 'what now?'

Scobell, for once, answered indirectly. Unconsciously echoing Martiny's policeman he said as a matter of simple fact:

'Criminals' wives are always vulnerable.'

Judie Shay's enemies when Jack was in prison were restlessness and finally boredom. She was ill-equipped to cope with either. Criminals' wives in the ordinary way were sometimes flashies or often mice but in either case had their private world, an established circle of other women with common difficulties but common interests. Judie had kept apart from it since both her tastes and her background were sharply different. She suspected that she was considered stand-offish and regretted what in fact was false judgement, but these women as women had nothing to say to her and the coincidence of a husband in prison was inadequate to bridge the gap.

Not, she had sometimes thought with a smile, that she wasn't at least as amoral as they were. Shay had told her he was a criminal and at first she had shied away from him startled, but he'd seemed practical and very quiet with the air of the solid professional man, and if his profession was breaking safes it was astonishing how soon one changed from shocked surprise to a cool acceptance. Besides, life in Portrush had been very dull. Her parents had kept a boarding house though they always called it a private hotel, one much patronized by week-end golfers since you could find a meal at any time. Her maiden name had been Judie O'Neill, but as often happened in Northern Ireland the name had said one thing, the background another.

47

Judie hadn't a drop of Celtic blood and her father was a passionate Orangeman. If Jack Shay had been a Catholic opposition would have been fervent and final, more violent than if her father had known that her fiancé's profession was breaking safes. In fact he hadn't discovered till later, when as a sensible man he had kept his mouth shut.

Sensible like all his race, but it had hardly been an exciting life for a girl who had guessed there were others less dulling. Jack Shay had had that London air, the excellent but casual clothes, the way he looked at her as the local men didn't, as a woman who clearly attracted him but neither slyly nor dropping embarrassed eyes. He'd attracted her too and the goad had grown; by the time they were married she was wildly in love. By now that had mellowed to steady affection, and loyalty was in her Ulster blood.

Moreover she had learnt the rules, which in her husband's world were both strict and humane. When your man came out you were always there, to leave him while he was in was contemptible, but equally you were not expected to live like a nun while he served his time. If your husband came out on a Monday morning your friend would go out on the Sunday night and he took care not to leave a shirt behind him. No other man would whisper a word, and as for their women she didn't know any.

This morning she almost regretted it, aware that an increasing boredom was only a step from outright victory. There was the shop of course, but it wasn't enough. You couldn't talk to a shop, you could only run it, and in any case there was a competent saleswoman who resented it if you breathed down her neck. Judie looked at her watch: it was ten o'clock. At eleven but not much before it she could take out the Mini and pay her first visit. There wouldn't be any problem of parking. One thing about the

48

much abused police: the locals knew who you were and were mostly helpful. Give them your name and they'd stare, then smile. The younger ones would sometimes salute. They'd put your husband inside—they were paid to do it— but it was beneath their sense of what was seemly to clobber his wife for improper parking. Once a Warden had but someone had killed it. Of course you mustn't be stupid on double lines, but that apart you might be the mayoress, though certainly you were much more attractive.

She walked to a mirror, disposed to confirm it, and her reflection looked back with a cool reassurance.... Not bad for thirty-two, not at all. She had the skin of a woman a decade younger and clear grey eyes under straight black brows. Her hair had the sheen of natural health. She wore it short and had been tempted to grow it, but the overtones of the tangle-haired miss were still distasteful to Judie O'Neill of Portrush. Small bones and an excellent figure. A woman. A shrewd little pussy? Perhaps. But a woman.

She made herself coffee and sat down again quietly. Boredom was a denial of life and she'd long since decided she'd know only one of them. She could live without having a man in her bed but men could stimulate as no woman could and in any case she knew very few women. It was stupid to pretend about men: the fact was that if you didn't have one you were only half a woman at best. No doubt you would have to pay for his company, but a great deal of rubbish was talked about sex, both by those who pretended you'd die without it and the others who asserted harshly that unless some priest or civic functionary had murmured his mantra before you indulged it the deed was inexpressibly wicked. The rules of her husband's world were more sensible. It was loyalty which mattered, not bed.

49

And Paul Martiny would know those rules. She was conscious that she attracted him strongly, he had taken her out to dinner twice, he'd sent flowers and been politely attentive. No more for the moment, he didn't rush things.

And she herself? The omens were good. Paul Martiny had what Jack had had too, the air of a wider world but more so, the throwaway manner, the understatements, the sudden and wholly effective smile when words would have muddied communication. Moreover his marriage had broken up. No, that wasn't true, it hadn't broken. Paul's world had its rules as hers had too and he wouldn't walk out from a wife and three children, a wife who had done him no wrong but fail him. But he was forty and he was very male, and a man of that world wouldn't do what Paul did, managing the affairs of thieves, if convention were his god and mainspring. In fact she had made her own decision that Paul Martiny was a secret rebel. He was too clever to express it openly, laying about him with impotent words, but he thought little of the world he'd been born in. It was boring and he didn't forgive it.

More important, he could bring her alive. He told her things, he could make her think, and the price for that was not exorbitant.

She went to her desk and looked at her diary. In a week she'd be going down to Cyprus, to the flat which Jack had bought and given her. Paul hadn't been needed to fix that flat nor his cousin who was a merchant banker. Cyprus was in the sterling area and the purchase had been perfectly open. In fact it wasn't strictly a flat but half a house in a Kyrenia suburb. Jack had known that she loved the sun and the sea and he was nothing if not an indulgent husband.

As Paul might be the perfect lover till this husband came out and resumed his rights. Paul knew her world's rules and would make no difficulties, no demands which she'd never consider conceding. Next time she saw him she'd talk about Cyprus, not inviting him there, he'd think that naive, but telling him of her own departure, then later, but in the same conversation, mentioning that the hotel was excellent. The service by air was frequent and fast and as for afterwards, if there were an afterwards, she knew that he had a room in London. Come to think seriously it all fitted perfectly.

She was considering this happy and apt concurrence when the doorbell rang and returned her to earth. She was surprised to hear the sound of it for the newspaper and the post had arrived and the milkman left her pint at the back. She wasn't expecting a visitor unless it were a collector for charity, and of these she had grown increasingly wary, the people from Oxfam and Christian Aid, a lesser host at their hungry heels. A generous woman she'd given generously till an African with a lah-di-dah accent had read her a lecture which lasted too long on what he'd foolishly called her obligations. His country, he'd said, was the object of genocide by brutal soldiery from the barbarous north. She hadn't answered him though she knew an answer. Instead she'd excused herself politely.

She had decided to do so now as she opened. It wasn't a coloured man but a red-head. He stood holding a hat with a gamebird's feather and a sports car had been parked by the kerb. Judie Shay couldn't place him except he looked spurious; she waited for him to speak and he did so. His voice matched the feathered hat precisely.

'Mrs Shay?'

'That's my name.'

'I'd like to have a word with you.'

She wasn't yet frightened. 'I don't buy at the door.'

'And I'm not selling things.'

51

'Then what can you want to talk about?'

'About that paper your husband left with you.'

She hadn't the least idea what he meant; she hesitated—a bad mistake. The young man pushed past her and closed the door. He stood with his back to it, smiling confidently, turning his horrible hat in his hands.

Judie was making herself think quickly. This man wasn't police and he wasn't a blackmailer. Jack had told her of those though he'd doubted they'd trouble her. He wasn't considered a violent man but had the reputation he could look after himself and by implication that he'd avenge a wrong. Besides, this red-head wasn't smooth enough for anything approaching the squeeze. If he had been she'd have temporized and then she'd have rung the police at once, the action which Jack had insisted was best. The police hated blackmail worst of all. But if the man's ploy wasn't blackmail what was it? He had the air of a strong-arm but that made no sense. No criminal in his normal senses left large sums in his house, with his wife, alone. This man wouldn't beat it out of her since she simply didn't have it to give him, and if he were what she thought he might be he would know that just as well as she did. Nevertheless he had scared her now; she would have to find out and that might be dangerous.

'Sit down,' she said.

The young man sat down.

She had decided that the best course open was to rush her fence boldly and hope for safe landing. 'What was that about a paper you want?'

'You know perfectly well what I mean.'

'I don't.'

'Oh come.' He smiled his confident, rather ugly smile. 'Since you know all about it there's nothing to hide. Your husband blew a safe and stole money, which is nothing

52

whatever to do with me. But the safe contained a paper too and that paper is very much my business.' He held out his hand. 'I want it. Now.'

'I don't know what you're talking about.'

The young man rose and went to the telephone; he ripped out the cord and returned to his chair. 'And now,' he said, 'you'd better be sensible.'

Judie had made up her mind. 'All right.'

'You've got it?'

'What do you think?'

'Then bring it.'

... Now comes the crunch. If he follows behind me ...

But the red-head was still grinning confidently. He didn't move from his chair as Judie rose.

She went to the bedroom and unlocked a drawer, then she took out the largest handbag she had.

In the sitting-room she sat down again, but she slid her chair back three feet before doing so. The handbag was on her lap and she opened it.

The young man was staring down at a gun.

The red-head didn't believe it—he couldn't. Criminals' wives never carried firearms. It was a rule of the trade and she'd broken it. She'd moved too far away to risk a snatch and he didn't fancy a wound from that weapon. He wouldn't have cared to try to date it. First World War, he fancied, and quite a piece. There'd be the hell of a bang and the hell of a hole. You wouldn't have very much stomach left if that hand howitzer caught you squarely. And that was what it would probably do. She knew how to hold it sensibly too, with both hands, as a woman should —no fooling. That way she wouldn't jerk, she'd squeeze, and the ambulance men would be mopping the mess up. That is if she hadn't done it first. She looked cool enough for even that.

53

The smile was now wan and distinctly uncertain. 'You wouldn't risk it,' he told her.

'That's for you to decide.'

A silence till he said: 'I've decided.'

'Get up then, but don't move closer. Stand.'

The young man rose.

'Turn your back.'

'Oh God.' It was the red-head who was frightened now.

'Walk to the door.'

He walked.

'Now open it.'

'Not in the back,' he said. He was shaking.

'Open it, man.'

He opened it.

5

He opened it and two men came through fast. One shut the door behind him crisply, the other said: 'Judie, what's going on?'

She smiled at Martiny but didn't answer, watching the man with his back to the door. The Chief Inspector was thinking quickly, his eyes going round the comfortable room. They took in the torn out telephone wire, Judie's gun and the red-headed young man. Who was standing looking square and stocky but his confidence had ebbed away. Judie was suddenly sure of one thing, that each man was aware of the other's profession and that the knowledge embarrassed them both about equally. The policeman began to speak politely. 'I'm a police officer,' he told her mildly. 'A Chief Inspector if it happens to interest you.'

'Won't you sit down?'

'Later on if I may.' He was talking to Judie but watching the red-head, talking while he made his decision. She hadn't attempted to hide the gun, but he looked at it with what was almost indifference. 'Have you a licence for that, Mrs Shay? A tiresome question, I know, but I'm bound to ask it.'

As answer she handed the pistol across to him. He tried

to break it and the first time rust stopped him, but as his forearm tightened the gun came open. It was unloaded and the firing pin was filed flat with the bolt from which it once sprang.

'I see,' the Inspector said, 'I see. As it happens you still need a licence for this, though I don't say I don't think the law is a hass. But only last year a man got twelve for waving a plastic toy in a hold-up. Of course he was working a crime—you aren't. And in any case guns are not my thing.'

He was thinking they were not his business and was privately delighted they weren't. On the contrary life might often be easier if more stout-hearted women pulled guns at intruders. Provided, of course, they were quite unserviceable, as this one very certainly was.

'You have three choices open and it's my duty to tell you. You can try and get a licence. You won't. Or you can hand it in at any police station when there may or may not be awkward questions. Or you can sell it to an authorized dealer as the near-antique it appears to be. His receipt will be your good discharge.' He was talking to make time, still thinking. It was evident that useless fire-arms weren't one of this Inspector's interests, and all the time he was watching the young man hard. 'You,' he said finally. 'What's your name?'

The red-head didn't answer him and the Inspector didn't press the question. He'd remembered again in Martiny's car that criminals' wives were always vulnerable, to the jackals, the vultures who often preyed on them, but this red-head hadn't the air of a jackal. He had the smell of something very different and the Inspector didn't approve of it. He'd have admitted that men like this were necessary—in the world as it was they were more than that— but the admission didn't outweigh his contempt for the
56

type of man who accepted the work. If his guess were right and experience backed it this man would be something to do with Security, and the circumstances and the man's appearance suggested he didn't descend from the top of it. Still, if he were any kind of Security a policeman would do well to walk delicately.

He began to feel a cautious way. 'Did you pull that phone out?'

'Yes, I did.' The voice was aggressive but the manner belied it.

'Malicious damage. Why did you do it?'

'Isn't that obvious?'

'Yes, it is. Forgive me a foolish question again.' The Inspector turned to Judie Shay. 'What did he want?'

'A paper.'

'Not money?'

'Perhaps he did but he didn't get round to it.'

'What sort of a paper?'

'I don't know that. He said it was something my husband had. So I went upstairs and fetched that gun. He was leaving when you arrived, you know.'

The Inspector said: 'Extremely timely,' then he looked at the young man again. 'Would you care to explain?' he asked. 'Just the framework.'

'I can tell you that I'm not a criminal.'

'Oddly enough I'm prepared to believe you. What are you then?'

'I'm not a policeman.'

'I really didn't suppose you were. But on the face of it you've been breaking the law. I *am* a policeman. Next move to you.'

'There won't be any other move.'

'Care to bet an even tenner on that?'

For the first time Martiny intervened. He had knowledge

57

the Chief Inspector hadn't and above all things he wanted to talk to Judie. He said smoothly: 'Perhaps there's been some stupid mistake.'

The Inspector smiled, he was sure there hadn't, but the banality was by no means unwelcome. He was hard on the hook and well aware of it, faced with a very awkward decision which he didn't desire to make in haste. A Chief Inspector was an important policeman but this was anything but straightforward police work. What he wanted was to talk to a senior, to the Branch which was really equipped to decide, and Martiny's remark, which sounded stupid, might in fact be a very helpful one. He sat down at last and looked at Judie.

'Apart from pulling out your telephone did he threaten you in any way?'

'If you mean did he hit me, no he didn't.'

'Menaces?'

'Not expressly—no.'

The Inspector was now at his crisis and knew it. In a carefully neutral voice he said:

'Then do you wish to charge this man?' He could see that she'd looked at Martiny behind him and he guessed that Martiny had shaken his head. For Judie said quietly:

'No, no action.'

The Inspector smiled, on top again. He spoke to the redhead. 'You'd better go.'

'What are you going to do?'

'Take instructions. I don't know what way they are going to break but I'm perfectly sure that I know where to find you.'

'Thank you,' the young man said.

'For nothing.'

When he had gone Judie Shay made coffee, slipping into the kitchen to do it, believing the two men would wish to

58

talk. In fact they sat in a total silence since the Inspector didn't wish to commit himself until a specialist had cleared the signals and Martiny wanted to talk to Judie, alone and not with a policeman listening. 'A paper which my husband had' would hardly have escaped the Inspector, so if he pursued this affair at all he'd return and start asking embarrassing questions. 'Paper' would strike him as maybe significant: Martiny, who had the background, knew it was. This young brute must have come from the man who had signed it, the man who had framed Jack Shay into prison and had somehow to get back what he'd written or face disgrace and very probably worse. To Martiny the morning's events fell in place but he'd have to talk to Judie Shay before deciding what could be done to meet them.

The Inspector finished his coffee gratefully; he said to Martiny: 'Perhaps I could ring you.'

'That's very kind.'

'Then we'll keep in touch.'

As he went down the steps of the house he saw him, a man idling on the opposite pavement, leaning against a railing casually and buried behind a racing paper. That would be Mr Martiny's protégé, the man he had hired to watch the house. The Inspector smiled but he didn't accost him. There were complications enough without risking more. He went on his way a thoughtful man, delighted that others must make the decision.

In the house Judie Shay was asking Paul: 'Do you know what that was all about?' There were times when her self-possession nettled him, when it crept to the edge of calculation, but now he was simply grateful she had it. He'd decided at once he must tell her everything, she wasn't a woman to play with half truths. But first there was something to clear between them.

'That paper you spoke of—you really know nothing?'
'I was telling the truth,' she said. 'Why not?'
'Jack didn't mention it?'
'Nothing at all.'
'He took it when he did that American. He gave it to
me for safe-keeping. I have it.' He liked it that she didn't
question him, no fussing about the inessentials. 'At first
I didn't open the envelope but I did when I heard a very
strange story. It came from another source, not Jack.'
She nodded composedly. 'I heard one too and it did
come from Jack. He told me that the last job he did had
been fixed to put him away for a bit. I didn't pay too
much attention, all thieves get like that in some degree. It's
not a persecution complex, or it hasn't gone that far with
Jack just yet, but they're suspicious and Jack's also proud.
It went against the grain to get eight and be left with a
bag of Indian silver.'
'I didn't pay much attention either but I did when I
looked at that paper of Jack's. It's a very dangerous paper
indeed—dangerous to the people who framed him. They
did that because they'd connected him with the job on
the diplomat's safe where it was. For all they knew he had
opened and read it and his knowledge could blow them all
sky high. Their first action was shutting his mouth by
prison and their next was to come to his wife for the paper.
Naturally they know nothing of me.'
'It adds up,' Judie said at length.
'I'm afraid so.'
'But there are a couple of things I still don't follow. First,
how did you know that man was here?'
... She looks like a woman, a very attractive one. She
thinks like a thoroughly logical man.
'When I read that paper it scared me cold. I put a man
on to keep an eye on your house.'
60

'That was really rather more than you owed us.'

'No it wasn't. I take my ten per cent.'

'And nothing more than your ten per cent? Never?'

It was an opening but he wasn't yet ready. She still had another question unanswered. He waited and she duly asked it.

'And the second thing is, why bring the law?'

'I didn't bring him, he simply came along. He was with me when the call came through from the man I'd put on to watch your visitors. Who didn't much care for the look of the last one so he rang me at the room I keep and the Inspector was there and talking business. Perfectly legitimate business.' He smiled at her, a colleague's smile. 'You know what I do to give me cover.'

'I know more about you than that,' she said.

Again it was an opening and again he wasn't quite ready to take it. It was a rule that business should always come first and mostly he had found it a wise one. 'So the Inspector decided he'd come along too. I could hardly have prevented him and in fact he handled the awkward bit for us—how to cope with a semi-official hoodlum.'

'What do you think he's going to do now?'

'I can't be sure but he won't act rashly. It was obvious he guessed where that young thug came from. The police hate their guts but they don't arrest them, or they don't unless they're actually forced to. That Inspector was very relieved indeed when you said you didn't insist on a charge.'

She laughed understandingly. 'I saw your face.'

'You think fast,' he said.

'A thief's wife has to.'

There was a comfortable silence as both relaxed. The business was over, let battle commence, the timeless and sometimes rewarding battle.

61

'Too early for gin?' she suggested.

'We've earned one.'

She returned with gin and tonic, smoking. Indefinably her aura had changed; now she wasn't the wife of the thief Jack Shay but simply a woman entertaining a man. 'I was thinking of going down to Cyprus, to the flat Jack bought. I've kept it on.'

'The sooner the better,' he said, and he thought so. 'I've a contact in Cyprus and he might come in useful. But it's a sterling area so I doubt if you'll need him.'

'You've contacts pretty well everywhere, haven't you?'

'If I hadn't I wouldn't be earning your money.'

This was perfectly true but he did earn his cut. Mostly he worked through his banking cousins, through his friends and the innocent old boy network which assumed he was accepting them, as certainly he himself was accepted, when in fact he thought they all stank to heaven and in any case were on the slide. The irony was an added incentive.

Paul Martiny asked her: 'What about money?'

'There's two hundred you pay my account every month. That's plenty and I even save on it. But I might see some local nonsense I fancy, so if you'd send out an extra three hundred pounds ...'

Not for the first time he felt relief. She had never demanded a large lump sum and if she had he'd have done his best to dissuade her. There were other men besides Paul Martiny who were interested in the affairs of criminals and one wife had once asked for thirty thousand. Her protector had been scared to death for he knew what the thirty thousand was for. She was going to try to spring her husband and that was a disastrous madness. Since he wasn't a high security prisoner there was a chance that such money could pull it off, but no sum of that kind could

62

be spent more unwisely. The risk of blackmail apart, who wanted it—a life on a nerve-stretching permanent run, every policeman directing foreign traffic a man who might have seen your photograph? Judie had never considered it and Paul was quite sure that she never would. She liked Jack Shay too well to destroy him.

Jack Shay who'd collected an eight-year sentence, unjustly no doubt to the legal purist but richly deserved for quite other good reasons. He'd always been a model prisoner, which meant that he'd earn his one-third remission, so Jack would be out in around five years, even less if the Parole Board were helpful.

Paul looked at Judie Shay and smiled, for the first time that morning a shade uncertain. She powerfully attracted him but he wasn't a conceited man and he knew that if he attracted her it was for what he could give her outside her bed. He couldn't just crawl into that and then drop her, she wasn't another girl in a restaurant. It was going to be an affair—he mistrusted them. Nevertheless she had offered two openings and now a third feeler was reaching out delicately. He knew that this was the final one: when he left her it would be Yes or No.

'So I'm going down to Cyprus next week.'

'That'll be fun as well as sensible.'

'The flat's rather nice.'

'I'm sure it is.'

'I prefer it to the hotel myself, though they say it's very good in its way.'

'I've never seen Cyprus,' he said.

'You should.'

'I've every intention of doing so soon.'

George Amyas had dismissed the red-head, furious though too well trained to show it. He knew that superior

63

thieves had protectors and this man who'd arrived had most clearly been Shay's. But the fact that he'd brought a policeman with him was on the face of it a dangerous complication. George Amyas, as Scobell had thought, had bought time to manoeuvre. It was now running out.

He looked at a written report on his desk. Mrs Shay would be leaving shortly for Cyprus.

He frowned for he hated personal action; he was a desk man who passed down the orders to others. He didn't dare to do that a second time, not when a policeman had come along too. They would play with you so far and then they'd rend you, they'd co-operate but their toes were tender. They might not go after that red-headed fool, but if anything similar happened again they would act because they would have no choice. Dropping a name, Jack Shay's, was one thing, a matter across a table at lunch, but violence in a policeman's manor was something you couldn't clear in advance.

Reluctantly Amyas picked up the telephone. He bought a first-class return to Nicosia.

6

It had been a very bad day for Peter van Ruyden. His ambassador had sent for him and in effect had warned him to watch his step. James Scobell had betrayed no private confidence but the organization which discreetly employed him was nothing if it wasn't efficient and rumours had dribbled in from London which its seniors found highly disturbing. It had passed these rumours, or some of them, to a man whom even an Excellency could hardly afford to ignore entirely. As a result he had sent for Peter van Ruyden.

But it wasn't the kind of interview which this kind of Excellency very much fancied. To begin with he hadn't been fully briefed, just instructed to warn van Ruyden sharply and van Ruyden would understand the import. Secondly he wasn't a career diplomat but a wealthy man and a politician, and though as the latter he wasn't re-markable as the former he'd helped his Party generously. Some of his friends were also van Ruyden's, not personal friends but men of that world. For van Ruyden himself he had no time whatever; he thought him as queer as a four-dollar bill. In this he was in fact mistaken, but to a man who had made his own money the hard way van Ruyden's air of fastidious elegance was a bullfighter's goad in a

65

good bull's neck. Still, there he was, he had background, connections. He would have to be handled with circumspection. No sane politician made enemies pointlessly. His Excellency knew how to handle men and he believed he could handle this playboy van Ruyden.

He recited his theme on a very quiet note, not disclosing that he had firm instruction to warn van Ruyden extremely firmly, but taking the line of an older man advising a younger of notable promise but a promise which could be cast away ... van Ruyden was a professional diplomat, a man with a fine career before him, one who also had advantages which most other colleagues didn't have. In diplomacy money was always useful and when near the top it was almost essential. Then wasn't it foolish to risk all this, to take chances by playing with other men's fire? The phrase had been suggested from Washington. The ambassador held a hand up and smiled. No, he wasn't prepared to answer questions, he had said all he wished and he thought it sufficient. He very much hoped it would prove sufficient.

Peter van Ruyden left him, furious. He had much more respect for the working diplomat than he'd ever had for a man like this. He had money no doubt, but it wasn't the old sort, he wasn't at all like van Ruyden's grandfather. You could never rely on parvenus. Never.

Van Ruyden walked across to Chancery where he asked for a week's special leave and was given it, then he caught an early afternoon flight to New York. He had made his late evening appointment by telephone, troubled less by his ambassador's words than by the fact that he had uttered at all.

Julius van Ruyden received him quietly. He was sitting in an invalid's chair, stiff and very upright indeed, dressed with a studied deliberation in the style of around the middle Twenties. He wore a high hard collar with rounded points and his hair, which was thick still though now quite white, was parted and plastered down from the middle. A severe dark tie and an old-fashioned tie pin. The pearl in it might or might not be real. He looked like a hard-working middle-class clerk in an age which had gone and would never return. He was one of the world's ten richest men.

He was also very near to death.

'When you telephoned, Peter, you spoke of advice.'

'I've had a warning from the ambassador.'

'Yes? A specific warning?'

'No, quite general.'

'Then I can't pretend I'm entirely surprised. We're a degenerate people but we're not yet incompetent. Our Intelligence is still quite good. What we've lost is our will, not our expertise.'

'But what will he do?'

'That gasbag? Nothing. One day he'll have to come home again and he's a very ambitious man indeed. That kind walks an endless tightrope and he won't chance a move to upset his balance.'

'And the State Department?'

'Won't risk a scandal. Nor will anyone else and those are our aces.'

The old man looked at his only grandson, not perhaps with affection—he seldom felt it—but certainly with a real respect. This was a proper van Ruyden, a real one, not like his disappointing father who'd been a teacher in an eastern College, had called himself a radical liberal and had supported that public farce and outrage which had named itself the United Nations. He hadn't wanted the van Ruyden empire and his father had scarcely mourned his death. In the companies which formed the pyramid

67

were dozens of efficient directors, hundreds of highly skilled executives, but the man at the top was a van Ruyden or nothing.

This boy knew it too and had been willing to help. Whichever way the old man's plan broke he was bound to lose his official career, in disgrace perhaps or just quietly resigning, but he hadn't given that a thought. The old man smiled, almost warmly now, thinking of all the dead van Ruydens. They'd been ripe, he supposed, for an intellectual but the poison hadn't touched his grandson. And he didn't believe he desired his death. All he wished, as the heir apparent he was, was the throne intact when his turn came to take it. Against that a career in the public service was something of no account at all.

But intact—he had helped to fight for that. There were meddlesome Trust Laws and men to enforce them, clever lawyers who waged an endless war with his own whose legal cunning protected him. But you couldn't plug every crack for ever and recently one had been widening ominously. To the old man it wasn't a crippling sum, he had put it at ten or perhaps twenty millions, but his lawyers hadn't been optimistic. And he knew where the twenty millions would go, on rebuilding some ghetto he'd never seen or on firing a ridiculous rocket at a target no sane man would wish to visit. He thought both objects of equal futility.

It had been typical that he had made his own plan, not changing his law firm nor fussing weakly. Instead he had grasped at the nettle directly. Behind every law stood the man who worked it, and like every other mortal man they were more vulnerable than the laws they lived by. And the Departments they worked for were even more so. The hands on the levers of power were human.

They were human enough to avoid a great scandal, they

would pay any human price to do so. That Report—it was useless to any Intelligence: the old man knew that just as well as Scobell. But it wouldn't be going to any Intelligence, it would go straight to the desk of a hard-pressed President who'd suffer most things before another Press savaging.... An American diplomat caught out meddling, not the C.I.A., which was known, often tolerated, but a man who had had no business whatever to be playing a game which belonged to others and using private money to do it. That alone might be something less than fatal, a matter of protest from high-minded persons, a scandal but one to be ridden out. It was where the money had come from that mattered. Van Ruyden money. The secret state. That lifted it into domestic politics, into a sensitive and explosive issue. Those van Ruydens were at it again. No, no, no. The Left would roar in frustrated rage but much more than the Left would join the chorus. There were millions of perfectly sane Americans who believed that to concentrate power was wrong. They had learnt that in their nurseries where van Ruyden had been a bad word like emperor. Nepotism. The hidden hand. Who could know who was next in line for corruption?

Julius van Ruyden smiled again. He was remembering a President who counted votes as a missionary counted converts. So he'd do most things to avoid their loss and one would occur without conscious thought. He'd take the heat off this hard old man in his chair. A word here, a word there. That was the way the real world worked and that was the way it always would.

Julius van Ruyden returned to his grandson. 'And how does the major matter stand?'

'Not too well. I got that Report but then I lost it.'

'How did you lose it?'

'My safe was blown.'

69

'That was bad luck,' the old man said. Strictly this wasn't his private opinion. A chance burglary was no doubt bad luck, but if a man didn't make his own luck he invited it. Julius van Ruyden and the first Napoleon would have agreed on one thing if nothing else: the good general was the fortunate one. Determinism was a word for highbrows but at a practical level it worked out the same. The successful man was lucky, true, but he attracted his luck as a magnet caught filings.

'But I think I can get it back.'

'From whom?'

'From the wife of the man who blew my safe.'

'You found out his name?'

'Not for certain at first but I'm certain now. An eminent safeblower went to prison for a crime on which he was caught red-handed.'

'That does sometimes happen.'

'Yes, I know that. But all he got from this job was some trashy silver, and stealing rubbish wasn't this man's form.'

'You're suggesting that he was framed?'

'I'm sure of it.'

'By Amyas of course—he had urgent motive.' The old man thought it over, then nodded. 'I'm inclined to think you are probably right. So you'll concentrate on the man's wife?'

'Who else?'

Old van Ruyden concealed a tolerant smile. This boy was a van Ruyden all right, but he didn't yet own a van Ruyden experience. 'I heard you call this safeblower eminent and eminent criminals' wives have protectors. Do you think you could deal with a man like that?'

'I can try. I'm certain the woman still has the Report.'

The old man in the chair didn't think this proven but

he also thought it entirely irrelevant. 'So you'll work on this woman directly?'

'Yes.'

'I'm not certain that is really wise. I think you have your priorities wrong.'

'Then who is the first priority?'

'Amyas.'

'I'm not sure I follow.'

'It's perfectly simple.' For the first time the old man moved in his chair, leaning forward in emphasis though it hurt him to do so. 'George Amyas will be a frightened man. *If he gets that Report back we'll never see it.*'

The impact was immediate but it was the impact of a fresh idea. Van Ruyden had not yet grasped what followed. 'You mean that if he gets it back he'll be too scared from what's happened to hand it over?'

'That's precisely what I had hoped to convey.' The voice was ironic but short of anger, though secretly the old man was irritated. He hadn't a great deal of time to live and men who thought slowly were wasting that little. Van Ruyden asked finally:

'What do we do?'

'I should have thought it followed fairly clearly. To obtain that Report is still important but it's more important, as things have broken, to make sure that George Amyas doesn't recover it.'

'And how do we do that?'

'One way.'

There was a silence till Peter van Ruyden rose. 'I'll think it over,' he said but he didn't intend to. He had no temple but his family's interest but the gods in it didn't include straight murder.

A servant showed him out of the house, returning to the man in the chair. He was kept alive by two male nurses and by an elderly coloured manservant. He knew the servant's name but not the nurses', who came and departed, mere paid automata. The old man rather resented them, but between the tycoon and the ageing negro was the understanding of two ancient men.

'Time for bed, sir,' the servant said. It was midnight.

'Not yet.'

'Doctor said——'

'To hell with the leech, where I won't be employing him. Bring me some whisky. Three fingers. No ice.'

'You've had your day's drinking.'

'I know that well.'

The old gentleman sipped the neat Scotch with pleasure and later his servant helped him to bed. But he didn't sleep, his mind was racing. There was that Senator who had married his grandniece, or that General in the Defence Department who was known to be increasingly restive. He had only his pay but seven children. A directorship here, another there ...

All these were possibilities—he'd think about them more clearly tomorrow. He'd decided the original project was finished, hinting at killing with a dying man's irony. And by any normal calculation the decision would have been perfectly right, the irony, after a moment, recognized. What upset both was in fact an accident. Literally an accident since Peter van Ruyden walked straight into violence.

He had left the house in the high east Fifties, one of few which were still in private hands, in a muddle of sharply varied emotions. What had swum to the top had been disappointment. To Peter van Ruyden the old man in the chair had been a symbol of all things he most respected, continuity and the old sound values. There were men who thought as van Ruyden did whom he couldn't

72

respect and even disliked but the man in the house in the high east Fifties had been a torch in the gathering night of decadence.

And he'd calmly suggested a cold-blooded killing. It would be proper no doubt to make proper excuses: he was really very old indeed and it was known he was now over-fond of the bottle, but character was immutable and even when old age came down an Olympian shouldn't suggest plain murder. When he did it let you down with a bang and it was also in its way an affront.

Though Peter van Ruyden didn't know it he was walking towards much worse than affront, into injury and un-relieved indignity, and to a man of Peter van Ruyden's background the indignity was as bad as the wounds. Or rather as bad as all but one.

He walked out of the house and looked around. When you needed a cab there never was one, and he turned left along Lexington, walking south briskly, enjoying the muted but sharp excitement of a great city which was partly sleeping. He was making his way to West Forty-Fourth Street, to his lodging which was also his club. He had affection for this extraordinary hostelry, the dust in the corners, the suspect plumbing, above all things for the superlative seafood. He went right at Forty-Seventh Street, then left again down Vanderbilt Avenue. Where Forty-Fourth met it he'd almost be home.

And behind the Hotel Roosevelt they got him. He could see at once that they weren't professionals. For one thing this area was still safer than most, and though he'd looked over his shoulder twice the gesture had been one of caution, not the reflex of a real apprehension. For another they didn't look like regulars. The men had long hair and Che Guevara moustaches, headbands and very heavy boots. The girl was clearly as high as a flag. He could place them, they

73

were people he hated, the kind which was eating his country's integrity. The three of them barred his way but were silent.

Peter van Ruyden stood still and waited. He hadn't the least idea what to do. If these had been professionals he'd have followed advice already given him, which was to hand over quickly and cut the loss, hoping that no worse would follow. But these were anything but sensible thieves, they were people with motives much less predictable. Van Ruyden said at last:

'What now?' He was a man with several serious defects but one thing he wasn't; he wasn't a coward.

The girl began to laugh hysterically. 'Oh Christ,' she said, 'that terrible voice. New England prep, it says, then Harvard.'

She happened to be entirely right but her intelligence was not reassuring. Van Ruyden looked back at the girl with horror. She might have been twenty-three; she looked forty.

One of the men said: 'Bastard. Fascist.'

It was a word which Peter van Ruyden detested. Ninety-nine men in a hundred who used it had no idea what a fascist was. It was a term of vulgar abuse like bugger. Come to that he'd rather be called a pederast.

He heard himself say: 'And what makes you think so?' He knew that it wasn't a wise remark.

The first man said to the other: 'Behind him.'

He moved and Peter van Ruyden waited.

The first attack came from the front, a blow. Peter van Ruyden could deal with that. He knew nothing of up-to-date unarmed combat but he could dodge a crude swing and he did so now. He stepped inside and hit out himself. The first man went down on his back, mouth bleeding.

The other behind him used his cosh.

The girl had begun to laugh again. 'Give to him,' she said. 'Let him have it.'

Van Ruyden had staggered but hadn't yet fallen. At the second and harder blow from behind he went down on his back, eyes open but helpless. The girl said again: 'Let him have it.' They did so. The first man had risen, kicking savagely, the second had knelt to flay on with the cosh. The girl had her heel in van Ruyden's face. She put her weight on it and ground it cruelly. 'Power to the people,' she said. He just heard her.

There was the sound of approaching feet, then shouting. 'Beat it,' the girl said.

All three were gone.

He did not know how long it had been till consciousness returned to him but when it did he could see he'd been brought to a nursing home. There was the air of scrupulous fussy cleanliness and a nurse in a chair quietly reading a paperback. The book had a lurid alarming cover, two hoodlums clubbing down a third man who was helplessly trying to shield his head. Van Ruyden could see it but not in focus. Something seemed to be wrong with his sight.

He didn't need the paperback's cover to jog his memory into instant action. He remembered what had happened clearly but he didn't immediately call the nurse; he had run into an accident skiing and he knew the form in expensive clinics. Show the least sign of interest and they promptly sedated you. A sedated patient was much less trouble so they kept you that way till the last moment possible.

He wanted to think before they doped him and his brain was coming back to life. But first he had to assess the damage. One leg was hung up in a kind of cradle and he could feel that his ribs had been put in plaster. He could move his arms and did so cautiously. They were painfully

75

bruised but nothing seemed broken. And he knew now why the nurse's paperback hadn't come into proper focus as usual. His head was heavily bandaged up and a side of the tangle came over one eye.

As the tide of conscious thought returned he knew that he hadn't a great deal of time. He'd learnt that from the accident skiing, the moment of extraordinary clarity before the pain caught up with the racing brain and you accepted the drug they were eager to give you. He gave himself at the most ten minutes.

His first thought had not been a bitter rage but almost one of indifferent irony. His grandfather had crashed from his splendid pedestal but that ambassador had been wholly right. Van Ruyden had left the house in the Fifties persuaded that his advice had been sound. . . . Killing indeed! The old man was senile. But it was practical till he died at last to serve on where a man had been called to serve. . . . The Honourable the Minister, in time perhaps even an actual Excellency. These were far from positions of feeble impotence, one could keep one's beliefs and even advance them. Putting it at the very lowest there'd be somebody to hold the brake on when some matter of national interest was threatened, not by force, they hadn't yet come to that, but by some woolly-minded idealist to whom *realpolitik* was a dirty word. These were the hidden enemies and it wouldn't be an ignoble life to devote a career to confounding them quietly.

He had decided that as he left the house but now the decision had gone with the wind. It had been a sound way to think but not to feel, and it was emotion which now unashamedly ruled him. 'Power to the people,' that girl had said as she ground her heel in his helpless face.

She had probably been some parlour anarchist without the least idea what that state would mean in terms of

76

quotidian human suffering, the stereotype of the mindless rebel which in communist states did corrective training in the tougher sort of labour camp.... Irrelevant, an over-refinement. She was as dangerous as any Party Member, more dangerous since without his discipline. But her challenge was at bottom the same, the collapse of every established value and with it of the van Ruyden world.

So the old man had been right, he was back on his pedestal. Against malice all means were entirely legitimate. Beware of distinctions without a difference. One could distinguish between a Commissar and the people who called themselves liberal humanists. One could do so but it obscured reality. Basically it was all one conspiracy.

The pain was catching up on him but these moments of almost god-like enlightenment were too precious to waste in some dulling drug. The mood of a quiet acceptance returned. The old man had known best, all means were proper, and if recovery of George Amyas's Report meant logically the death of Amyas then his death would be one like uncounted others. Peter van Ruyden now saw that clearly but he also saw clearly he couldn't do it. Not wouldn't, just couldn't; he wasn't the man. He hadn't been trained in the arts of killing. He was useless really, those drop-outs his betters. At least they had dared to act. He didn't.

He was ready for the nurse and called her, and she rose at once with her clinical smile. 'I'll ring the doctor,' she said and used the telephone.

Peter van Ruyden could see from one eye that he was the sort which practised in rich men's nursing homes, polite to a point which was almost deference but as detached from actual human suffering as though it wasn't sickness and pain which earned him a very good living indeed. 'So you're conscious,' he said. 'That's good. Don't

77

talk.' He held up a hand. 'I'll do the talking. You were beaten up but in a way you were lucky. A bone in your foot and three ribs cracked. Concussed but there's no frac-tured skull.' His smile was almost as bright as the nurse's. 'Any pain yet?'

'Yes, it's coming back.'

'I'll give you something for it.'

He did so. The needle slid into van Ruyden's arm and he lay back relaxing, his unbandaged eye shut. They thought he had gone but he hadn't quite. Through the fog as the drug bit he heard them talking.

'Bad luck about his eye.'

'Yes, very.'

'It was done by the heel of a woman's shoe. It was hope-less, of course. We had to remove it.'

'When will you tell him?'

'He'll find out soon enough.'

The doctor went off on his prosperous round and the nurse stood staring at Peter van Ruyden. Now that the patient couldn't see her she allowed her professional mask to slip. It was a crime, it was something really wicked. To half blind a man and not even to steal from him, just violence for violence's sake, a shame. She looked down at Peter van Ruyden with pity.

The emotion did the nurse high credit but at this moment it was wholly misplaced. Generations before the nurse's grandparents had escaped from a pogrom in east-ern Europe a hard and hungry Dutch younger son had set sail from the Hook in a craft he mistrusted. The van Ruydens still had his Bible to prove it. They didn't read it a lot but there it was, all succeeding van Ruydens entered meticulously, chronologically under the first one's name. They didn't read it a lot but they heard it read for they still went to church and sometimes they listened. Evil was not to be suffered indifferently. A tooth for a tooth and an eye for an eye.

So the nurse looked down with shame and pity but now looking at an authentic van Ruyden. The blood had become a little thin, generations of wealth had cut its vigour.

Not any longer—no, not now. The hard and hungry Dutch younger son was alive again in this wreck on the bed. The nurse couldn't guess it and far less know. She was looking at a total stranger.

7

Martiny had spoken of visiting Cyprus but as he woke in his bed in the country next morning he realized he hadn't entirely decided. It was one thing to take what the kind gods offered, quite another to accept a commitment. Commitments meant complications—he loathed them. It wasn't a question of right and wrong but more importantly of what was decent. He had a solid respect for Matty still, conventional though she was to distraction; she could drive him insane but he didn't dislike her. And he hadn't had to marry her, it had been an alliance just as much as a marriage. Her parents had been neighbours of his and he'd known she'd inherit a good deal of money. She had accepted it as perfectly natural when most of it had gone into his land, modernizing a run-down estate into a well run and quietly prosperous business. He paid her six per cent on the loan but she might easily have lost the lot if he hadn't had modern ideas and training. If she had she would never have grumbled—never. Matilda never nagged at him, a virtue he wasn't inclined to minimize. All she did was simply to bore him stiff and as a woman she was cold rice pudding. He resented it that he slept in the dressing-room but he didn't find expatriation intolerable. Be fair, he told himself, be just. You weren't obliged to

80

marry her, and brought up as she had been she hadn't a chance. If she thought you had other women (she did) then that, after all, was quite conventional provided it was also discreet. Probably she was relieved in secret since bed, she'd made clear, was a duty, not pleasure. So a room in London was quite in order but humiliation would certainly not be. Nor would he consider it. It wouldn't be fair and it wouldn't be decent.

There were also the children though he liked them unequally. His elder son he didn't much care for; he thought him a bit of a snob like his grandparents. Michael was twelve, at a fashionable prep school, and sending him there had troubled Paul. But what could one do in this day and age, at a time when the balance was visibly trembling but hadn't yet fallen on either side? The local school was known to be terrible with a headmaster who was a posing theorist. Paul Martiny could have swallowed this if only the man had been good at his job. Unhappily he clearly wasn't. The school as a school had a very bad name, and on a simple choice of unwelcome evils a private prep school had seemed by a whisker the lesser. Just the same it was stamping Michael wickedly, the stereotype of the English gentleman, and moreover he was a mother's boy.

It was different with Patricia, his first born. She was a cool fourteen, mature, a young woman, and Paul Martiny adored her blindly. She repaid him with a shrewd understanding, perhaps, he sometimes dared think, with love. They never spoke of her mother, they didn't need to, but Paul knew that she had her mother mustered. When Patricia felt the need of some fun she came to her father and quietly suggested it. That was excellent for a parent's ego, and come to that it did him no harm as a man. And he'd been fortunate with Patricia too since he hadn't had to

81

send her away to some barracks for young ladies of fashion. There was a convent school near, where she went as a day girl, for the Reverend Mother had been much to Paul's taste.... So neither parent was a Catholic? That meant they would have to pay full fees. Paul had said gently he thought he could manage them. The Reverend Mother, who smoked in private, had offered him a cigarette.... And Protestant was an imprecise word. What sort of Protestant was he, please? He had answered he was an old-fashioned one, the sort who was prepared to protest.... Excellent, that was just as it should be. She had respect for the sort of Protestant who burnt the Bishop of Rome in annual effigy. What she couldn't abide was those damned Anglo-Catholics.

So Patricia was growing up happily and he hoped that the baby would do the same. At the moment he was less than promising—even the way he was sick was patronizing. Martiny smiled as he thought of the baby. He'd been taken for an imperial ride but he didn't resent it, he thought it funny.

He'd been astonished when his wife had suggested it, but there she had been as bland as butter, calmly suggesting another, an afterthought. He'd been astonished but it was also a challenge, and there were arguments which she didn't need put. They had Michael and Patricia no doubt, but by the time they were sixty both would be married, very probably with their own young families, whereas if she had one now and she knew she could he'd be twenty and keeping the pair of them interested.

I am old, he had thought, and the young are my teachers. That was fashionable exaggeration but it could save you from the unconscious arrogance which an old age too freely accepted brought down on you. As for Matty it was a good investment, like lending her money on Martiny's land.

He owed her on that more than six per cent.

He had thought it over and then said Yes, but making a simple but firm condition. If they did it at all they'd do it properly, no sneaking into her bedroom one night. Instead he'd fly her down to Venice.

And he'd never seen her before—she understood him?

All right, if that's how you want it. You're crazy.

He'd been hoping he wasn't entirely that for he'd heard stories of women of thirty-six who unexpectedly woke like the Sleeping Princess. Matilda Martiny did no such thing. To begin with she didn't take to Venice, it was hot and it smelt and the Lido was vulgar. And she said all the wrong things without knowing their wrongness, or more fairly she seldom discovered the right one. There was an eminent English *littérateur* who would have approved of Matilda Martiny's taste; she liked the pointed arch and stained glass splendours, and the villas of the Veneto, which Paul thought the finest buildings on earth, left her cold as a gothic cathedral left him. And as for a second honeymoon, it hadn't been so unlike the first. To do her justice she'd been extremely gracious, at rare moments she had even been charming, but she hadn't been the awakened Princess, simply a woman who wanted a baby. He had felt like a racehorse at stud and behaved like one.

And back at home it had still been the dressing-room. He had rather hoped it mightn't be but at least she had never made a promise. Matilda wouldn't, she never lied. If he'd taken the hook he'd done so knowingly, and the baby would be a compensation.

He finished his morning tea and shaved, then he went to his study; he wanted to think. He wanted to read that Report again and he pulled it from an inside pocket. He was carrying it on his person now—Shay wasn't the only man who blew safes and in any case his own was old-

83

fashioned. He had considered his bank but had turned that down. Banks weren't wholly secure against the law and to deposit it would be admitting possession.

He'd never had James Scobell's expert knowledge so the paper had never struck him as worthless, something which any competent embassy could have produced at a six-hour notice or less, an opinion which a political journalist would probably have on his spike already. His anger rose as he re-read the words for they struck him as a simple treason and a *trahison des clercs* at that. This Amyas was the typical clerk however high up on his ladder he'd crawled.

Paul Martiny fetched *Who's Who* to check him. George Arundel Amyas, born 1916. He skipped the next five lines to read the end. Amyas had been a Deputy Secretary in the Ministry of Social Security but was seconded to the Foreign Office for work which wasn't expressly stated.

Paul Martiny smiled, it was clear as the dawn: George Amyas was high in Intelligence, or perhaps he preferred to call it Security. The distinction today was paper thin. This entry wouldn't deceive a schoolboy, far less a foreign agent who'd know, but it was a tradition in a decaying establishment that it didn't admit that such things existed. They weren't orthodox and were therefore suspect. *Ergo* you couldn't list their heads, though everybody who mattered would know them, *ergo Who's Who* bore this foolish entry.

But he was less interested in the concealing absurdity than in the details of the man himself. He turned back to the earlier lines and frowned. George Arundel Amyas, born 1916. Apparently father was Canon of somewhere and his mother had been a bishop's daughter, the sort of respectable High Church background which the Reverend Mother had roundly detested. Moreover it hardly suggested wealth,

84

so fifty thousand English pounds would be a fortune to George Arundel Amyas.

Now the frown was a scowl for Paul wasn't satisfied. Corruption itself didn't raise his hackles, there were parts of the world where it greased the wheels, but though most men of Whitehall would lick anyone's spittle provided he paid in promotion and honours it was rare to find an ape of this jungle who would sell out his masters for hard cold cash, especially the ape called a Deputy Secretary. Such a man would be thinking of knighthood, not money.

Paul Martiny liked to have motives clear and he didn't believe that George Arundel Amyas would have written this paper for money alone. To a poor man, as Amyas probably was, fifty thousand would be a serious factor, but there'd have to be something else. There must be.

He decided that it was probably simple, recent history turned neatly inside out. The precedent was indeed outstanding, an establishment man as George Amyas was, a man who had risen quite high in Security. And for almost the whole of his working life he'd been betraying his country's secrets to Russia. That was true but it was also inadequate. Not to Russia so much as the Marxist ideal. What had bitten this man was the religion of communism, but there were committed anti-communists too and not all of them were merely absurd. Some were—he had heard them talking absurdly.... If you must fight two wars in a single man's lifetime, two wars on what a child could see was clearly the wrong side to fight on ...

Paul Martiny shook his head. No, not that. George Amyas would be much too intelligent to be frightened of bolsheviks under his bed, but suppose that the virus had really taken, suppose he saw it as that other man had, as a matter of ineluctable duty.... Your country was weak and it wasn't reliable, in any real crisis it would feebly

85

back down. Then it was a matter of conscience to help the hard ones, do your duty by the men you could trust. You must tell them how the British Cabinet would react when the chips were really down, that if China went into North Vietnam the Foreign Secretary would storm and bluster but collapse at the first real hint of pressure. To do so would be logical and also it was a righteous deed. That was the word for dedication, the word for a man who was grimly committed.

Paul Martiny laughed aloud at the irony. This Report had been going to cost fifty thousand and it was fifty thousand pounds too much. A man who had read George Amyas wisely could have had it for precisely nothing.

He turned from considering Amyas to the action which he had now made necessary. For Martiny couldn't just let things run: Judie would be at risk indefinitely, and whether or not he recovered this paper Amyas could write it again. God rot the man, the man was a traitor. There were circles where the word was unfashionable, people who were more interested in the psychology of a twisted mind than in the damage which it had done their country. Paul Martiny wasn't one of them. He managed criminals behind his cover, honest criminals who mostly despised all politics, but a traitor was outside the pale and all the fine writing of intellectuals ('There are worse things to betray than a country') couldn't change him from what he was, nor his infamy.

Paul Martiny lit his morning cheroot. He mustn't succumb to indignation, it wasn't his business to punish Amyas. He could do so perhaps, but the price would be scandal, and that would defeat his primary object. Which it was difficult to express unpompously, all the words in this field sounded worse than stuffy. But he hadn't a moment's doubt what it was. Paul Martiny who took ten per cent on the earnings of several high-class criminals was determined to do a good citizen's duty. The only question was how. He considered it.

He wished he knew more about high Security, but all he knew was what he suspected, that it wasn't the least like what spy stories told him. And it went against his blood to duck, to slough off the problem on somebody else who in dealing with one of his own queer kind might start with his hands half tied behind him. He knew a man at his club who he was sure was Security—not George Amyas's lot but more senior and subtler—but he was on anything but firm ground himself. Take this paper to any sort of official, a high one or just the ordinary police, and they'd be obliged to start poking about, asking questions. How, for instance, had Martiny acquired it? That was the last thing Paul wanted looked into.

He started to draft a careful letter, deciding he wouldn't expressly reveal that he actually held what George Amyas had written. That would take off the pressure from Judie Shay but it might also bring it down on himself, and though that didn't frighten him he was frightened of what he knew was his ignorance. In this world you had to be very careful lest a casual slip wreck the hand completely; and behind all the doubts of a world which was strange was the recognized fact that his own position wasn't such as to invite inquiries as to how Paul Martiny, landowner and noted do-gooder, had acquired what was certainly stolen property.

He tore up two drafts but passed the third, which was a very formal affair indeed and written on paper he seldom used. A man like George Amyas would take note of the writing paper.... Mr Paul Martiny presents his compliments to Mr George Amyas and has information which he believes might interest him. It concerns a certain docu-

87

ment. Mr Martiny would be pleased to discuss it, of course at Mr Amyas's convenience.

He suspected it read like the first move from a black-mailer, but it might also be what he hoped it would sound like, an excessively pompous country gentleman who was writing to a total stranger and was studious not to appear familiar.

When George Amyas read it he didn't think it familiar. He was more frightened than he had ever been. He looked at his diary for reassurance. He was leaving tomorrow for Cyprus. Good. He had only one means to save himself and very little time to do it.

Paul Martiny mostly decided quickly but for a week he'd been bogged in indecision. On the one hand he wanted Judie Shay and he knew that if he went to Cyprus he'd be unlikely to be wasting his time, but on the other he'd be committing himself to something he'd never indulged before, a continuing, almost a formal liaison. He'd de-cided now as he packed a suitcase but the decision was one which he still mistrusted. For he'd taken it for the worst possible reason, in a fit of frustrated irritation. No doubt it was understandable but by now he should have learnt to live with it. More precisely to live with the woman he'd married.

Just the same it had been vintage Matty. The baby had an excellent nurse and Matty had heard him crying one night. She had gone to look and there they had been, the nurse and a man in the nurse's bed.

Matty had made a thing of it, excoriating a tolerant husband. Not that he didn't partly sympathize—you shouldn't bring men to the house you worked in. The nurse's affairs were her own, not theirs, but certainly they should be handled discreetly. But Matty hadn't seen
88

it like that, she had ground on about reliability. Fornication might be all right today but the fact remained that it wasn't *trustworthy*. The nurse must be dismissed at once.

She was not dismissed, she was much too valuable. Martiny had fixed it but only just, and the interminable discussions had bored him. Finally they'd agreed a compromise. Paul would have the nurse up to his study formally and would reprimand her with all severity. In fact he had offered a glass of Sherry and had had difficulty in keeping it serious. This he hadn't told Matty, nor had the nurse. It was the only bright spot in a squalid affair which had otherwise flayed his nerves to tatters. Matty wasn't an evangelical, it might somehow have been easier if she'd been struck by some dotty revelation, she was simply a cripplingly conventional woman.

Which wasn't, he thought, as he went down the staircase, his suitcase in one hand, his hat in the other—which wasn't a very respectable reason for sneaking away to Cyprus and Judie.

But he walked to the waiting car with decision and the driver stowed the bag away. Martiny's estate had survived by efficiency, and one of the new necessities for any well run and also paying land was that the holding should be some sort of company. So the house was the manager's perquisite and the manager was Paul Martiny, two gardeners were paid as cowmen, and the chauffeur (Paul never called him that) was carried as the estate mechanic. It was a fiddle and therefore deeply satisfying, a spit in the eye to the powers that be. Not so satisfying as managing criminals but a gesture of happy contempt just the same, a small thread in a hidden rebel's pattern.

In the station yard he saw Matty's small car, which surprised him since he'd said his goodbyes, but he knew that she sometimes lent it to neighbours, in particular to the District Nurse. She was a great one for every kind of good work and was friendly with the wife of the vicar. Who was also a very stupid woman. He corrected himself: Matty wasn't stupid; she had simply never flowered and never would.

But on the platform she came up to him, a little uncertain and almost shy. He had only once seen her shy before, on the night he had carried her down to Nice, and he remembered this now with a flick of conscience. Nevertheless the air became her. She was a well-made woman though far from fat—Junoesque, he decided, would be the literary word. It was difficult to imagine her diffident, but she came up to him now with less than assurance.

'I thought I'd come and see you off.'

'That was really very kind of you.' There was nothing else to say so he said it. The 'kind' had sounded absurdly formal but one didn't say 'sweet' to Matilda Martiny.

The train came in and he opened a door. He was carrying his suitcase himself since he hated displays of menial service. He leant out of the window, feeling foolish. Suddenly she pulled his head down. She kissed him, not with passion but warmth. 'Have a good time,' she said. 'You've deserved it.'

It was the nearest Matty Martiny would come to what he realized was a sincere apology.

At the airport a bus took him out to the aircraft and at the head of the gangway a stewardess smiled. The smile held more than professional welcome. Paul Martiny was a type she fancied, lean and unmistakably male. Paul smiled back but was not responding. Flirtations with air girls were not his taste, a form of casual titillation which he'd decided was at least as frustrating as that Bunny Club he'd been taken to once. The place had nearly made him vomit, more salacious, he'd thought, than any Striptease and with the same result in the end. Which was nothing.

The aircraft began to move, then stopped. They waited for perhaps five minutes and for once the loudspeaker spared them banality. The stewardess was passing again and Martiny raised a hand. She stopped.

'What's the trouble?'

'A passenger.'

'You mean you're holding the flight for a late one?'

She nodded and looked out of the window, pointing a painted finger briskly. Her nails were blood red and Martiny loathed them. A jeep was approaching fast with a man in it. It also had an extensible ladder.

'He must be a very V.I.P.'

'I wouldn't know but it certainly looks like it.' She glanced at a list. 'We're only one short. The name's George Amyas. Do you happen to know him?'

'I don't,' Paul said but he thought: 'Not yet.'

8

Paul rang Judie after breakfast next morning, but early as he was he was second. She sounded delighted to hear his voice but she delayed his call with the casual coolness which at times he admired and at times found infuriating. 'Don't come just yet, I'm expecting a visitor.'

'As early as this?' It was certainly action. Paul had more than a hunch who the man would be.

'The name's George Amyas.'

'Is it indeed? Do you know what he does?'

'I can guess where he comes from,' she told him calmly.

'Then hadn't I better come up and help you?'

'I don't think so—you might frighten him off. We both of us want to hear what he says if only to clear the air a bit.'

This was a facer since undeniable. 'Have you anyone there to help in a pinch?'

'There's the gardener Zekky, he's eighty but Turkish. Do you think there's going to *be* a pinch?'

He considered that, fairly sure there would not. 'No, nothing at all like that fuss at your house. George Amyas is above all that but he'll be capable of turning nasty.'

'I didn't know you'd ever met him.'

'I saw him on the same flight out here and he didn't

look quite my idea of a crony. Also I've read what he writes. I don't like it.'

'Then if he brings another hard man I'll bang the door in their faces and ring you at once.'

'I'll accept that,' he said since he knew he would have to.

'And I'll tell you what happened this evening at supper. I sleep like a log in the afternoon so come up about six and in time for a drink.'

She settled to wait for Amyas, in no way disturbed by Martiny's warning. It might be awkward but it wouldn't be violent, and if it were she could call to Zekky. The maid was a Greek—quite useless, naturally. Greeks could hide behind walls and shoot people down, or put bombs under babies' prams in cantonments, but when it came to anything face to face they would run and discuss it ardently afterwards. Every race in the Mediterranean basin had handed them out some form of beating, and if there was an admitted exception that exception was Mussolini's Italians which didn't prove much and maybe nothing. But an old-fashioned Turk wouldn't stand for a fracas. If his employer called out in fear or pain he'd come running and he'd be ready to fight. Zekky happened to be a great-grandfather but he was also a very tough old man.

The bell rang and Judie answered it, inspecting the man who stood outside. 'Come in,' she said, 'and please sit down.'

'Thank you.' He did so; he sat and waited. As gamesmanship she thought it ham and she could see what Paul had meant on the telephone when he'd said that this rapidly fattening man was not his idea of a personal friend. He wore a tropical suit and a spotted bow tie and he was trying her out with the oldest trick. If she started the talk then he'd count it one up. She had never heard of

93

Martiny's *trahison des clercs* but knew a successful clerk when she saw one. Amyas might be high in his strange profession but he wasn't so very different from the man who did her shop's accounts. Paul Martiny would explain it better but she hadn't a doubt that her instinct was right. Her instinct and what she saw before her, a self-important but secretly insecure man.

When she'd won the first battle of silence he spoke. 'It is kind of you to receive me, madam.'

She reckoned now that she'd read the form: he'd start on a note of extreme formality, then switch suddenly to covert menace. This would be the interesting bit—any menace depended on power to back it. She didn't believe that he held such a power but she meant to find out and to tell Paul Martiny.

'What can I do for you?'

'Help your country.'

'Really?' she said.

... My God, but he's pompous.

'I'm concerned with Security. That's my job.'

One tiny mark for 'job', not 'profession'.

'I don't think I've ever put it in danger.'

'You haven't but your husband has. He blew a safe some months ago but I assure you I have no interest in that. Not as crime—I'm not a policeman. But the safe held a very important document and your husband took that away as well. Since your husband's in jail for a different crime he can hardly have that document with him, so I'm certain you have the paper yourself or at any rate know who holds it and where.'

'You make it sound very simple.'

'It is.'

'Is that why you sent that man to my house?'

She gave him a second mark for not ducking. 'A mistake,' he said coolly. 'Sincere apologies.'

'There happened to be a policeman present.'

'I know there was, I've been told of that. It was reported to me but that will end it.'

... He's trying to show me how powerful he is.

'I told your man I knew nothing about it.'

'You must forgive me, madam, if I don't believe that.'

'Believe what you like,' she said and waited. It was an invitation to lead a card. He tried one.

'A young man of mine broke several laws. A policeman was present. Nothing has happened. Does that mean anything to you?'

'It does. It means that I declined to charge him.'

'They could still have proceeded.'

'But they didn't.'

'Just so.'

'If you're trying to prove that the police will play ball with you it's something most people would guess in advance.' She decided to offer a lead herself. 'But I don't have to guess myself—I know. My husband doesn't steal bits of silver.'

He didn't rise to the bait but she knew he'd seen it. His manner had begun to harden. 'You're putting my own case for me strongly.'

'The case that you're people who'd stick at nothing?'

'Since you put it like that.'

'Oh, go to hell.'

It was provocative and meant to be. She wanted to see his real hand, not the openers, but the effect was much more than she'd ever have guessed. He began to breathe audibly, his pot belly swelling, and she realized she'd gone further than goading, she'd wounded where it hurt severely. Thieves' wives didn't talk like that to officials.

95

Without intending to she had cracked his carapace.

'You're much stupider than I thought you,' he said. 'Being stupid can be extremely dangerous.'

There was nothing to say so she didn't say it. He was going to show his hand at last.

'State papers are a serious matter. If you don't realize that it's my duty to warn you. Everything is stacked against you.'

'The power and the glory?'

'You're foolish to play with me.'

'Then please tell me why.'

He didn't do that: instead he rose. 'I'll give you just twenty-four hours,' he said.

... Just as I guessed, he holds no aces. Nothing but the hope to scare me.

'At this time tomorrow, then.'

'If you must.'

'Till then au revoir.'

'I'd prefer goodbye.'

James Scobell was smoking faster than usual. He was a seriously worried man, as close to being jittery as any man with his roots in good soil could be. He knew nothing of the affair at Judie's but more than enough of other matters to inhibit his usual sound sleeping at night. For instance he knew who had signed that Report, or rather he had made a guess which he regarded as a moral certainty. He had served in England for fifteen years and there were men who might think that far too long, but it had given him an unmatched knowledge of other operations in his private jungle. George Amyas was one of them and he reckoned he understood George Amyas.... The right wing intellectual—Jesus! They were as dangerous in their different way as the most venomous of the other persuasion and in anything which they believed important they'd be every bit as capable of putting conviction before their simple duty. Or so James Scobell sincerely thought. Van Ruyden had told him where he'd bought his Report and the signatory must be somebody senior if the paper was going to carry real weight. Say fifty thousand pounds of weight. So for Scobell's shrewd and experienced money the almost certain suspect was Amyas.

George Amyas who'd flown down to Cyprus. It hadn't been hard to discover that. James Scobell would have thought it amateurish to have put an active tail on Amyas, but it was known in the trade he was going away and for a fellow professional the rest had been simple, just a matter of using established contacts with the airlines and the bigger travel agents. And if it were asked why he'd chosen Cyprus when his holiday ground was the south of France, van Ruyden had mentioned the name of Shay, a safeblower caught with some valueless silver, collecting eight years for the crime he'd been caught on, one untypical of a top-class peterman. James Scobell had considered this worth an inquiry.... This criminal had a flat in Cyprus and his wife was spending the autumn there. So Amyas had gone down to talk to her, to threaten or to persuade or buy, but by some means to get back in his hands what was now far too hot to leave outside them.

By itself this would perfectly suit Scobell. The danger of that absurd Report lay not in its secret—there hadn't been one—but in the fact that the name at the bottom was Amyas. If that came out there'd be serious trouble and James Scobell disliked it heartily. Privately he mistrusted George Amyas but he was an animal in Scobell's lush pasture where it was an axiom to co-operate, even, when one could do so, with enemies, and where peace and over all things silence were the essentials for any fruitful work.

Amyas didn't stand high in the nameless hierarchy, not one of the three or four who decided, but it wasn't a world of watertight bulkheads. An upheaval would affect them all. Scobell had spent fifteen years in building, trust and co-operation and liking, but the fire of a really serious scandal could send that up in smoke in a day. And an American diplomat would have sparked that fire, no American would be trusted further. No more lunches in that club in Pall Mall, the hints which were better than formal statements, the shrugs which contrived to answer questions. These men weren't stupid; they were also officials. They wouldn't want to know Scobell.

So if Amyas got his paper back that would be fine for James Scobell. Like the old man in the house in the high east Fifties he was convinced he wouldn't now dare to sell it. He'd renege on his bargain and burn his paper. He'd be too frightened to do anything else.

When everything would be just as it had been, no fuss and no uproar, just priceless quiet. Scobell would still have the contacts who mattered, everything would be just the same.

He shook his head reluctantly for it was tempting to leave it like that and relax, sweeping it under a mental carpet. Unhappily it wasn't justified. George Amyas and that thief's wife apart Scobell knew something which really scared him; he knew about van Ruyden's grandfather.

When he'd heard that van Ruyden had flown to New York, suddenly, taking special leave, it had been routine to alert his own New York office, and van Ruyden had made straight for his grandfather. James Scobell frowned, fear close at his shoulder. Intellectuals mistrusted the phrase power politics, which to men like Scobell meant simply politics. What Scobell mistrusted was power misapplied. Unless the old man had broken up, and all the reports be-

98

lied that strongly, his interest and indeed his motives were mysteries still locked in his own white head.

And there was other and disturbing news, since van Ruyden had left the old man's house and had walked into a vicious mugging. The overblown solemn abracadabra of what was nowadays loosely called psychiatry was something which James Scobell detested, but one needn't embrace it to know something of men. Violence could alter their values, especially a violence which cost an eye. Some men it might simply break but it had been known to put a dangerous edge on what had previously been quite mild steel. Scobell did not admire van Ruyden, he thought he was far too smooth and worldly. But heredity was a word with meaning and with blood like the van Ruyden blood you could never be sure what would throw up next.

James Scobell scratched an ear in quiet perplexity. The facts he had were not conclusive, nor were they anything like reassuring. Van Ruyden had left the expensive clinic, discharging himself against doctor's orders, ribs fairly well mended but still limping heavily, and there would still be a second operation to clean up the mess which had once been his eye. If plastic surgery were fairly successful he'd be spending the rest of his life with an eyepatch. At the moment his face was still massively bandaged.

And this man who'd discharged himself, doctors protesting, had promptly taken an aircraft to Athens. He was known to have served there and spoke good Greek; he'd have connections or could easily make them. It was alarming that there was no news of his doing so. He had walked off the aircraft and disappeared.

Athens was very close to Cyprus, close geographically, close in ethos.

Paul Martiny had talked of a contact there but James Scobell had much more than that. He put through a call

99

and a woman's voice answered him. He began to talk in fluent Turkish and the woman's voice said at the end:

'We'll report to you.'

Paul Martiny left Judie's flat at dawn since the maid came at six and Paul was scrupulous. They had decided their business the night before, not too easily but at last they'd agreed. Judie for once had been less than rational, or less than what Martiny thought so. He'd had a day to think and now saw it clearly: George Amyas had declined his fly but as events had broken he'd now have to take it. Paul Martiny could oblige him to take it. He'd come up to the flat again next morning and they'd handle the cards from there as they fell. With that Report in Paul Martiny's pocket, if necessary waved at Amyas, there was bound to be a play for game, though what that play was going to be was something which depended on Amyas. But one thing was at least assured: a man who'd been bent would bend again.

To Paul's surprise Judie Shay demurred. She'd protested it simply transferred the risk, from herself to Martiny who hadn't earned it. He'd answered that he was prepared to accept it but Judie had started to talk of trouble. Trouble would spoil everything—everything. She hadn't defined what everything was but he'd arrived to begin an affair with her and Judie, for all her apparent calm, was a woman before she was criminal's wife. No woman would want an affair-cum-violence, the fear of a knock at the door, the tension; she'd want tranquillity and room to breathe, leisure to let her emotions flower. But finally he had won her over, not by argument but by what he was. Judie had wriggled but finally yielded. She knew one thing about a man like Martiny: if he'd decided there was an obligation then nothing a woman could say would shake him.

Very well then, come up tomorrow. We'll see.

So he was walking to his hotel, content, at ease in mind and relaxed in body. She had made him tea before he left and it was still early for the hotel's breakfast. He decided that he'd bathe instead, taking the lift to his room and changing, walking along the concrete pier to the sea-water pool and the sea itself. He swam strongly and always used the latter and he didn't give the pool a glance.

He was standing with his back to it, ready to dive when some instinct pricked him. It was the impression of another presence and he knew that he was quite alone. Nevertheless he straightened and turned, then he ran to the pool and dived in flatly. The body was fully clothed and bleeding, the water around it reddening darkly. It was floating on its face. He turned it.

It was the man he had seen on the aircraft, George Amyas. From the very faint bleeding he was only just dead.

9

Paul Martiny was considering lunch when the card was brought in on a silver tray. The inscription read *Mr Asterios Angelides* and the manager had brought it himself his manner a mixture of self-importance and an unease which he couldn't completely conceal. 'He's a policeman,' he said, 'and a very important one. He wants to talk to you privately, at once if it's possible.'

Paul Martiny was less than surprised. The formalities in the early dawn had been handled with astonishing smoothness, less astonishing, he reflected later, when you remembered that for a resort hotel the last thing desirable was bodies in swimming pools. He had run to the drowsy clerk at the desk and the clerk had promptly woken the manager. An ambulance had arrived discreetly and a policeman to take a very brief statement. All concerned had been Greeks with a common interest, never spoken but clearly overriding: the visitors mustn't know of this, or only so much as couldn't be hidden, and even that must be doled out later and gently; there mustn't be any sort of panic, no foreigners asking awkward questions—worse, deciding to leave and making scenes. The manager had put this tactfully and Martiny had been sympathetic.... Mr Martiny would no doubt realize that an affair of this sort could be very damaging. Moreover the police had a legitimate interest which might be prejudiced by precipitate action, precipitate meaning simply curious. Guests milling around the pool and gossiping, besieging the couriers who ran their tours. An impossible situation for everybody. Mr Martiny understood him? Thank you. I thank you very sincerely indeed.

So Paul went downstairs with the anxious manager, to a room behind the outer office. A man rose politely and the manager left them. The visitor smiled.

'My name is Angelides—it's rather a mouthful. Most of the English here call me Angel.' His English was very good indeed.

'Good morning, Mr Angel, then.'

Angel pulled up a second chair for Martiny. There was a third behind an impressive desk but Angel made no attempt to take it. They sat in their two armchairs, as equals.

... This man knows his business, I'll have to be careful.

Angel was watching Paul without seeming to. His impression was much what they'd told him already. All hoteliers were by training observant and the manager was his second cousin. Amongst Cypriots that made him one of the family and his opinion had been at once respected. Mr Martiny, he'd said, was an Englishman, apparently in comfortable circumstances though he didn't flash his money about, but the manager, who'd seen many English, considered he was a little different, some indefinable English difference. You would have to be born an Englishman to find any sort of word for it, but one couldn't run a resort hotel without realizing that this crazy race had an incomprehensible system all its own. So just say that Martiny was different and leave it.

Angelides, looking at Paul, agreed.

103

Paul Martiny, too, was inspecting Angel, but without benefit of previous briefing. He was quietly but very sharply dressed, his linen spotless, his shoes rather narrow, the Mediterranean man *par excellence*. He had rather more hair in his handsome nose than a west European would gladly have tolerated but otherwise was as carefully barbered as a contemporary American President.

'I'm sorry to be taking your time up.' He spoke Greek in his home but was almost bilingual and had also attended a police course in England.

'I don't know that I can help you much.'

'I'm rather afraid that may be true, but you found the body, I have to question you.' His manner didn't change as he asked: 'You knew this man?'

'I'd never met him. But we came out on the same aircraft together.'

'But you gave his name to the local sergeant.'

'Of course I did. I knew his name.'

'May I ask how?'

'By plain coincidence. The flight was delayed for a man coming late. The stewardess told me his name—it was Amyas. The rest was remembering faces—that's all.'

'Do you know his profession?'

'I don't know. I can guess.'

'May I ask how again?'

'There's a book called Who's Who——'

'I've looked at it. Just between ourselves I didn't need to. The name was quite enough for me.'

'You're something more than a policeman, then?'

Mr Angel smiled. 'I must strongly deny it. I hold a senior but quite orthodox rank and that means I have the usual knowledge. But I don't move in the late Mr Amyas's world.'

It was a matter of private satisfaction that the statement

104

was entirely true. Angelides was a professional policeman with the contempt of his trade for what were loosely called agents and something more than contempt for the word Security. Not that either was at all unknown to the man in black whom he loyally served, but they were directed not against visiting foreigners but the people which happened to share the island. Like all good Greeks Mr Angel despised them, but the emotion was also mixed with fear since whatever was said about racial majority the plain fact remained, bleakly inescapable, that if the man in black overplayed his hand this despised but also martial race could drown the island in a bath of blood. The soldiers of the United Nations? The Angelides smile would not have flattered them. They were hirelings from Scandinavia who wouldn't stand for a minute in real disturbance, far less in what might well be invasion. So naturally Security was a very important matter indeed though it wasn't Mr Angel's pigeon. But his own duty was at least as important and had been defined to him in subtle Greek which for once could be translated simply. It was to keep the island's nose quite clean since so much of its income depended on tourism. Nothing frightening, no scandal, nothing bad for publicity. A murder was certainly major scandal—it had happened and he could do nothing to stop it—but the English had strange ideas about justice. Since a man had been killed he must find a killer or there'd be something a good deal worse than scandal, an impression that the place wasn't safe, that murder could happen as it happened elsewhere but that the police shrugged their shoulders and let it go.

And clearly this wasn't an ordinary murder—George Amyas had not been an ordinary man. He'd been head of a part of British Security and the implications of that were extremely alarming.... Some vendetta from a world Angel

105

feared fought out on an island already vulnerable. His master wouldn't stand for that.

Angel stared at Paul Martiny again. He rather liked the look of him and he didn't believe he'd killed George Amyas. It would be a shame if he had to frame Paul Martiny. He said after very careful thought:

'So you knew what the late Mr Amyas did.'

'I told you—I looked him up in *Who's Who*. There's an entry which wouldn't deceive a schoolboy.'

'But you'd never seen him till he joined your aircraft. Did you look him up before that or after?'

It wasn't the expected question but a lie could be very risky indeed. Paul had been in Cyprus less than two days and he hadn't been near a public library. *Who's Who* wasn't a volume one took on holiday and for all he knew the hotel didn't have it. 'Before,' he said and waited quietly.

Mr Angel's reply to this surprised him. He nodded and smiled as though relieved and began to lay some cards down smoothly. 'In that case I've nothing to hide from you as clearly you're hiding nothing from me. There's a lady here called Mrs Shay.' He held up his hand as Paul started to speak. 'No, I beg you not to misunderstand me. Naturally I know that her husband's in prison but I've nothing against Mrs Shay whatever. She has adequate means and pays her bills, she's the type which is very welcome indeed. But you'll realize this is a very small town and it hasn't been in any way difficult to discover that you've already visited her. To be accurate you had dinner together.'

... The maid, of course. Paul Martiny considered. Kyrenia was indeed very small, and early as he'd left Judie's house there'd been people already moving about. He had no motive to conceal the rest which was also probably

106

known in any case. 'I rang her yesterday morning,' he said. 'Then I went up to dinner and stayed the night. I left very early before the maid came.'

If Angelides knew this he didn't admit it. Instead he bowed politely. 'Thank you. However I wish to make perfectly clear that I don't regard that as a matter of interest. Mrs Shay's private life is in no way my business. The same goes for yours if you'll let me say so.' Mr Angel inspected his well-kept nails. 'You say that you rang her yesterday morning?'

'I rang her to make the evening engagement.'

Mr Angel laid another card down. 'In the morning the late Mr Amyas called on her. May I ask if you had knowledge of that?'

'She told me on the telephone that Amyas had asked to see her.' This man was much too competent to risk lies which might be later exposed.

'Did she tell you his object?'

'Not in terms. We discussed the matter at dinner that evening.'

The next obvious question was clearly 'What matter?' and Paul hadn't decided how to answer. But Mr Angel had no intention of asking it. The late head of a branch of British Security had had business with the wife of a safe-blower and that could only be the sort of business which Angel would give a month's pay not to know. His duty was to avoid all trouble, not to meddle in a dangerous world where the outcome could be unforeseen. A killing was the worst publicity and he must mitigate that by finding a killer. The man in black wouldn't have it otherwise. Justice must be properly done and justice must be seen to be done. Local and quiet and he hoped soon forgotten. But international espionage—Security if you preferred the word—was the reverse of local by definition, and

Angelides could lose his job if he stirred up a hive which his master feared. That master would be more than scared, he'd be a very angry man indeed.... Agents fighting it out on his tourists' sun-trap. As though those accursed Turks weren't enough.

But he had one more question and asked it blandly. 'You went down to bathe and discovered the body. I suppose you didn't examine it?'

'No.'

To Angelides this was very important. When the sergeant of police had first arrived George Amyas had not been robbed. Mr Angel had discreetly robbed him, wristwatch and passport and eighty-three pounds. Motiveless killings were worst of all.

He rose and shook hands, polite and friendly. 'I'm really very grateful indeed. Are you staying here long?'

'Several weeks, I hope.'

'And I hope that you very much enjoy them. I don't think I need intrude again though you may have to give a more formal statement about finding the body—no more than that. The law, you know—it's tiresome everywhere.'

He went back to his office thinking hard, a man on a tightrope without a net.... George Amyas had been deep in Security and had had business with the woman Shay. Paul Martiny might know what that business was for his relationship with Judie Shay was lover and therefore quite probably confidant. But Angel was sure Paul was no sort of agent, though one of that kind must have killed George Amyas since no one else known had a motive to do so. Such a man would have slipped from the country by now, and in any case to discover him would be to stumble into a frightening world which Mr Angel, a good policeman, detested. But equally one couldn't let killings pass. It was bad enough that the thing had happened, it would be very much worse if the tale seeped around that not only were innocent Englishmen murdered but the local police had done nothing about it. Mr Angel had been on a police course in England, where he believed he had mastered the English mind. Its first assumption would be Greek incompetence, the second would be Greek corruption. The one thing the English wouldn't suspect unless he made some slip which suggested it, the one thing they wouldn't easily think of, would be framing another visiting Englishman.

Angel went back to his office frowning, opening the first report on his desk. He thought it unusual but not significant. Arrivals of any conceivable interest were noted as a matter of course, and if they seemed in any way strange their movements were discreetly checked. This one had been an American who'd come in on a passport beyond suspicion, but the Immigration official had been alerter than many and had noticed that the American's passport bore several diplomatic visas, not for Cyprus but for other countries. . . .

You are visiting Cyprus on holiday?

Yes.

You have a diplomatic visa for Greece where your aircraft has just arrived from.

Yes. You will notice that it has long since expired. I went back to Athens on holiday, privately, a matter of looking up several friends.

Van Ruyden had filled in a form on the aircraft and the official had looked at this form again. This American appeared to be booked at a respectable rather expensive hotel, though it wasn't the one most Americans went to. He'd had an accident, his head was bandaged, so he'd come here for rest and a little sun. He was carrying an Athenian newspaper, and since he had been *en poste* in Athens it was reasonable to assume he could read it. It was all quite in

109

order but it wasn't quite usual. The official's instructions were clear and mandatory: anything not quite usual went forward.

When a routine but also careful inquiry was made at the expensive hotel which the American had named as his. Since he hadn't checked in there the police had been interested, but visitors sometimes changed their plans and it wasn't until no other hotel had owned to a Mr Peter van Ruyden that the matter went up as high as Angelides. Who instructed a little testily that an American with a bandaged head should be easy enough to find.

They found him. He was found in a room in a middle class suburb, a sort of boarding house for the bordello next door. It was a very well conducted one, the best in the town and indeed on the island.

It was this saved van Ruyden from further police interest. Angelides had simply smiled. He considered this very peculiar conduct when there were notably better women in Athens, and for a man who had travelled first class on an aircraft, a man who could afford good hotels, to hole up in what was a sort of annex used by customers from Famagusta, from Limassol and places beyond (it was unheard of to sleep in the brothel itself) struck him merely as grievous misuse of money. But one had to make some show of tolerance for a people which hadn't even existed when his own had been something more than civilized. Moreover Mr Angel read widely, and though American novels left him coolly contemptuous one mustn't be sourly anti-American, the sin of the shallower intellectual. But the facts were there for sane men to observe and he flattered himself he had understood them. The *mores* of the American male were childish and sometimes actively barbarous but they were conditioned by their appalling women. A

110

man of an ancient culture should pity, not amuse himself with idle judgement.

He marked the file No Further Action.

As he did so Paul Martiny finished his lunch, then went up to his comfortable bedroom to rest. Judie had insisted strongly that an afternoon sleep in a climate like this one was something no sensible man forwent, and in any case he had risen early and at lunch had drunk most of a bottle of wine. He had discovered the local whites with pleasure after ordering an undrinkable red.

He opened the door and stopped dead, outraged. His room was in a total chaos, drawers opened and jumbled, his clothes on the floor. Even the bed had been stripped to the mattress and he began to remake it, cursing softly. Some hotel thief but an unsuccessful one. He always carried his money on him and he tapped his breast pocket to check it instinctively. His wallet was there with George Amyas's Report.

He lay down in pyjamas and was almost asleep when the squeak of the bathroom door disturbed him. He lay still but he looked at the bathroom door. It was opening, inch by inch, very slowly.

So the thief hadn't gone, Paul had simply disturbed him. He'd been hiding in Paul Martiny's bathroom.

He wondered what would happen next, less frightened than overwhelmingly curious. What was the form here? He didn't know. Suppose you played possum did sneak thieves just go? It was a first-floor room which faced the mountains and it was an easy drop from the balcony to the garden and the car park below. This thief had found nothing worth the taking but Paul's coat was now slung across a chair. He wouldn't lie still while some Cypriot rifled it, but if he showed that he wasn't yet asleep he might change what was a hotel robbery into something which could

111

end in violence. Alternatively if he just feigned sleep the man might simply cosh him anyway.

... I'll be damned if I'll let some Cypriot do me.

He sat up sharply. The door was open. A man stood framed in it, staring at Martiny.

Whatever he was he wasn't a Cypriot. He wore something quite like a good Sikh's turban except that one half of the head was unbound and no Sikh tied his puggree over an eye. The hair which was left uncovered was fair, too fair for this part of the Mediterranean, and the skin had a clear and Nordic pallor. The man stood silently, making his mind up, then he slipped into the bedroom quickly and stood at the foot of Martiny's bed. Paul could see he had noticed the coat, was deciding.

'Who in hell are you?'

The man didn't answer. He was looking at the coat, not Paul.

When he moved he did so surprisingly fast but Paul had got his feet down first. He was covering the chair with the coat, not considering violence, reacting instinctively. The man had pulled a pistol out but he was holding it by the barrel, to club. He swung clumsily at Paul and missed and Paul stepped inside, swinging too, with a fist.

To his astonishment the man went down—astonishment since in all his life he'd never had any interest in fisticuffs. He'd never learnt boxing or self-defence but the first time since boyhood he'd closed a fist, a grown man was unconscious across his floor. Beginner's luck, he thought, and grinned. He looked curiously at the hand which had done it. The knuckles were bruised but the skin was unbroken.

Paul Martiny sat on the bed and thought. This wasn't any sort of Cypriot, not a Greek and certainly not a Turk; he was probably a local Poor White, a man who had come here full of hope but who certainly hadn't achieved his

112

end. The good job once, then the good job lost. The second job not so good, the third. Begging from English tourists, then worse. Poncing and pimping. Humiliation. This man had had more than enough already.

Paul Martiny rose, his mind made up. He picked up the gun from the floor and unloaded it, holding the cartridges, frowning thoughtfully. He put them in a drawer and locked it, then he went to the bathroom and soaked a sponge. Returning he used it clumsily but the man was already coming round.

When he was conscious Paul helped him up. The fall had shaken him worse than the blow. He put a hand up to feel his bandaged eye.

'I didn't hit that,' Paul said. 'You were lucky.'

The man made a sound, half sigh half groan.

'And now you're going to be luckier still. Just get out of here and get out fast.' He handed the pistol over, smiling. 'No funny stuff—I've taken the cartridges. And if you're not beyond taking advice I should lose it. They give you much more when they catch you armed.'

Still the man with the bandaged eye didn't speak. He turned on his heel and walked to the window; he climbed the balcony's balustrade, hanging by his hands, uncertain. Paul had followed him—he'd looked dangerously shaky. But the drop was six feet or at the worst it was eight and there was a hibiscus bush in extravagant flower. Paul was sorry the man's fall would wreck it.

He let go at last and fell untidily, but he picked himself up and walked away. He looked back once and that was all.

Paul Martiny took a thoughtful shower, then went back to bed and slept two hours. Any further decisions he'd take at his leisure.

*   *   *

Peter van Ruyden had no idea of it but he wasn't the first man who'd cleared his mind and the high gods had laughed and thrown down their gifts to him. He only knew he was getting the breaks and he accepted them at their plain face value.

The first had been in the matter of Amyas, for he had flown into Cyprus in hope, not certainty. He'd told his grandfather he would work on Judie and had accordingly made the essential inquiries. Mrs Shay, he had learnt, had a flat in Cyprus and she used it most springs and every autumn. George Amyas must recover from her the Report which in other hands could destroy him, so if Judie Shay had gone to Cyprus then Amyas must be close behind her. There was a chance he had acted in England already but it was one which van Ruyden would have to accept, and on the whole he was inclined to think that a man in George Amyas's private dilemma would much prefer to bide his time till he could tackle his quarry away from her background, away from what his grandfather had spoken of as her likely protection. Van Ruyden felt sure enough of the logic but the timing of George Amyas's action was where the luck would come in and he'd need a good deal of it. It might be at once or it might be weeks. All he knew was that Judie stayed a month and he might have to wait for all of that.

But he hadn't been on the island three days, making a recce of Judie's home, when he'd seen George Amyas walk up to it openly. Half an hour later he'd left looking furious. So George Amyas hadn't recovered it yet and George Amyas wasn't going to recover it. Particularly not when he went for walks, late evening walks from his seaside hotel, in the dark by a now deserted pool.

Van Ruyden lay back on his bed and smiled, savouring what he knew was good fortune, and he'd had more which

114

he couldn't possibly guess. In Athens he'd gone to a girl he had known and the lady had not been displeased to see him; he'd been gentle and always paid on the nail, which was more than some of her clients did, and when he'd asked for her help she had given it freely.... He wanted to go to Cyprus, did he? but he didn't desire to attract attention. With his head bandaged up that mightn't be easy, and all visitors to hotels had to register. But she had a cousin in Cyprus, a girl in the same ancient trade as herself. Naturally he couldn't stay with her—that would be very improper indeed and her cousin would never consider it—but there was a house next door where men often slept and it wasn't what you'd call a hotel. The police knew all about it of course, but the police were also sensible men quite apart from the fact they were underpaid, and if Peter didn't mind some discomfort....

He had said that it sounded fine for his purpose and in fact it had been much more than that. An American diplomatist who had booked at a big hotel and not gone there, a man with a bandaged head who spoke Greek, were matters in which a good policeman like Angel would normally have shown more than interest. But such as he'd had he had lost at once when he learnt where Peter van Ruyden was staying. He had smiled a very Greek smile indeed, contempt in it but also pride. Contempt for this astonishing country (he couldn't bring himself to say civilization) whose males travelled thousands of miles for a woman, and pride that these men had the simple sense to recognize the best when they saw it. Greek tarts were that. They always had been.

Van Ruyden knew nothing of this but still smiled. For George Amyas's prompt arrival, the fact that he'd made the killing easy, weren't the only good breaks which the gods had thrown him. He knew now who had that Report. Not the woman.

George Amyas had not been her only visitor. Van Ruyden had been watching her house, since with Amyas unsuccessful and dead what he wanted would still be with Judie Shay and sooner or later he'd have to steal it. That would be better than scaring or bribing. George Amyas would have tried both and had failed.

And a man had come out of her house, an Englishman, not a man with the air of a casual visitor. So grandfather had been right again, she was a criminal's wife, she was being looked after. Manager, maybe lover, *protector*. He'd be holding the paper, not Judie Shay. Confirmation? He'd let van Ruyden go. Clearly he was afraid of publicity. Any normal man would have called the police.

So on the first occasion van Ruyden had failed, which was running against his luck but not breaking it.... I know where he's staying, he visits the woman. It isn't a very big island. It's on.

When he woke from sleep his eye was hurting, it had hurt off and on since he'd left the hospital. He didn't much like the look of it. It was hard still when he changed the dressing not to shudder with disgust and resentment but there was something much more than a horrible wound. He suspected it wasn't entirely healthy. Sometimes the flesh round the cavity swelled, as often as not it was soft and puffy. And when it did hurt it hurt like hell. In the clinic there'd been analgesics but he hadn't brought any out with him. What a chemist would sell him brought small relief but the girl in Athens had found him something. It worked but he knew that it made him light-headed. He couldn't use it when thinking of serious business such as holding up Martiny again.

But the pain apart van Ruyden was happy. The drug

which he'd got from the girl fought his pain and mentally he'd surrendered contentedly to the potent release of violent action. He'd never used any drug before and of the two he was taking the release was the stronger. His life had been lived in his disciplined mind, in his work and his hobbies, his porcelain and pictures. Now his mind wasn't disciplined, it was wholly anaesthetized. Why he wanted the late George Amyas's Report was something he hadn't considered for days. It was the finding it which mattered fiercely. That was enough, both reward and end. How it was used was for Julius van Ruyden.

But he wished that his eye didn't hurt so much, and those tablets the girl had given him weren't something which he dared take for long. A week perhaps—that ought to be plenty. A week to do what he'd really come for. Killing George Amyas had been a necessary preliminary, the mere removal of what had become an obstacle; the main objective remained, the Report itself. For Martiny that might well be disastrous but van Ruyden was not concerned with that.

He took two more of the Greek girl's tablets and so far he'd only taken them singly. They put him out in a matter of seven minutes.

10

Next morning Judie Shay drove Paul to the western point
of Cape Kormakiti, her little car bumping springs and
passengers along the alarming but beautiful corniche road.
It was a trip which she felt she almost owned, through
Orga and Liveras, still almost untouched by the tourist
hordes, through the bird sanctuary to the point and the
lighthouse. Here one coast marched east for the length of
the island, the other swept south into Morphou Bay.
There was a little eyot offshore, perhaps thirty yards dis-
tant, and between it and the baking blistered shore two
tides fought it out where their waters met. Both Judie and
Paul had brought bathing gear, for nobody travelled this
magical coast without the means to enjoy some enchanted
beach. Judie began to reach for hers but Paul put out a
doubtful hand.

'I wouldn't,' he said. 'Not here, at least.'

'Why ever not?' The single spit of sand was inviting.
Half teasing she added: 'I believe you're afraid.'

'You're perfectly right, that's the proper word.' He
pointed to where the two waters met. 'That's what yachts-
men call a race, I think. Or you could say I've a decent
respect for the sea. It's very much bigger and stronger than
I am.'

118

'But we both of us swim pretty well.'

'I dare say we do and I was born with a caul. Which my mother always used to tell me was a guarantee that I'd never drown. Just the same I'm not swimming here. Nor are you.'

He had said it with his easy smile but she knew that if she tried he'd stop her, and the fact that he was probably right was illogically an added irritant. He was charming and worldly, a resourceful lover, but he was also a very stubborn man. Perhaps it was something to do with his background. Convince him that some action was foolish and nothing another could say or do would persuade him that it was anything else. Conversely if he smelt a duty, something which touched his peculiar conscience, he'd pursue it without considering cost.

She returned to the car a little huffed, and they drove through Livernas, back to the bird sanctuary. In spring it would be beautiful, green with new crops and country flowers; at the end of the long and rainless summer it was beautiful still but with different beauty, stark and lean as any Ionian island. Here the sea was mostly out of sight, its presence immanent but seldom defined. They had started early at seven o'clock but by nine it was already hot, the dust rising in an occasional eddy. The carob trees were filmed with its powder like old windows in a deserted house and a dark smoke rose from the smouldering stubble. It was a land of subsistence farming, a hard one. Lizards darted away from the car's slow progress. There wasn't a human soul in sight.

Nothing human but the birds were there. Paul knew that the migrants were often limed, an intolerable and a barbarous business, but here even the natives bred in peace. There were more magpies than he had seen outside Normandy, a black and white bird which he didn't know, a

119

sort of sparrow dressed for a formal dinner, a hawk overhead which he watched till it dived. And once Judie Shay had to brake quite sharply—a hoopoe was sunning itself on the track, wings outspread in the dust and its crest collapsed. The gorgeous bird was safe and knew it, astonishingly reluctant to move. Judie laughed and finally blew the horn. The bird put its crest up and flew away, stripes flashing in the luminous sun.

'I've never seen one of those,' she said.

'Nor have I. There are stories they're sometimes seen in Norfolk but it's a curious place to go for a sun-lover. North Norfolk at that where it's pretty bleak.' He added a countryman's expert aside. 'Barley and sugar beet, dairying too. But the winter can last for seven months.'

'You love the land, don't you?'

'It gives me a living.'

'But you have to escape from it?'

'You should know that.' He kissed her hand. 'There are compensations.'

'A lot of them?'

'This is the first.'

'It must be nice to be established and rich.'

He said with a surprising emphasis: 'Being established is absolute hell. That's why I do what I do to escape from it. As for being rich, I'm not. Not by modern standards at any rate.'

'A lot of people might think you were.'

'Yesterday one thought me worth robbing.'

He told her about the thief in his room, lightly and as a casual incident.

'And you let him go?' She was indignant, it wasn't a sensible action.

'Why not? He was a down-and-outer.'

'Who had a gun.'

'He'd have never dared use it.'

'And you haven't told the police?'

'Of course not.'

She considered it very foolish indeed. As a criminal's wife she respected the police, the English police or any other. It was stupid to take risks with them, concealing other people's crimes when you hadn't a valid motive to do so. The gesture of letting a sneak-thief go had doubtless had its own panache but this wasn't a virtue most policemen were fond of. 'I think you're taking a risk,' she said. 'Suppose the police found out.'

'Suppose it.'

'Wouldn't they think it very odd? After all they've an interest in you already.'

'You mean that I found Amyas's body? The two incidents are unconnected.'

'To you they are but the police might not think so. I know pretty well how a policeman thinks.'

'You're exaggerating,' he said.

She was silent. She could see his point of view well enough, explicable in Martiny's world, but in her own it was alien, even dangerous. She shrugged for it wasn't worth an argument. Once already that morning he'd shown his stubbornness.

They drove through Orga, out of the sanctuary, on to the frightening coastal road. Here the sea was in constant sight and sound, sometimes two hundred feet below, the track snaking and bending, mostly sliced from the rock. On the right of the driver the wall was solid, on the passenger's side a sheer drop to the sea. The surface was loose and some corners blind. Judie drove very slowly indeed. 'Bad place to meet another car.' They hadn't seen one in the whole of the morning.

They were coming to the worst of the corners—she'd

remarked on it driving the other way. There was an up-hill approach over treacherous rubble, then a forty-five-degree swing right. The seaward side was unfenced and naked. There was a motorbike leaning against the rock.

'Lucky that isn't a car,' Judie said.

She was feeling her way with extremest caution, the steering juddering as the rubble rocked it. Behind them there was a very faint breeze and at walking pace or even less their own dust had begun to overtake them.

A man stepped out from behind the corner. He had a bandaged head and was holding a gun.

Judie Shay stopped the car and waited quietly.

Paul looked at her with increased respect. She seemed perfectly calm, awaiting instructions. The man with the gun came towards them slowly.

'It's the man I was talking about, the one who tried to rob my room.'

'What do we do?'

'Could you drive straight at him?'

She hesitated but only shortly. 'I suppose I could if you told me to. But suppose he shoots——'

'He didn't before.'

Judie let the clutch in fiercely and the man with the pistol sighted and fired. He shot at the offside tyre and missed but the effect was the same, Judie jerked the wheel. For a sickening second the car slid left, one wheel within inches of final destruction, then she over-corrected and swung to the right. The car hit the rock with a crunch and reared.

The man was at the open window. 'Out,' he said briefly. 'Out and quickly.'

The driver's door had buckled and jammed. Paul climbed out first and then helped Judie. The gunman was covering them both but shakily.

122

Judie noticed it first. 'He's drunk,' she said softly.

Softly but van Ruyden heard her. 'I assure you that's one thing I'm certainly not.' Just the same he knew that he shouldn't have taken it, not another of the girl's deadly tablets, but the merciless pain had come down on him cruelly. It was that or he couldn't have moved at all.

Paul looked at him. He was swaying dangerously. 'I don't think you're drunk but you're pretty sick.' He'd been listening to the accent carefully. It was educated eastern American, the last speech Paul had expected to hear. 'You're the man who broke into my bedroom yesterday.'

'And I still haven't got what I came for.'

'No? But I see you had some other cartridges and I still think that carrying guns is silly.' Paul was playing for time while he thought what to do.

Van Ruyden was not, he was shaking miserably. It was an effort to him to speak with clarity but he managed that and also menace. 'If you stall,' he said, 'I'll have to kill you.'

'Then obviously I shouldn't stall. Money?' Paul reached for his wallet. 'There's thirty here.'

For a moment the haggard face broke in a smile. 'I don't want your money.'

'Then what do you want?'

'The other thing in your pocket.'

'What thing?'

'Listen. You were right—I'm sick. I've been taking a drug and I'm not responsible.'

'What do you want?' Paul asked again.

'That Report from George Amyas.'

'Which you think I have?'

'I know you have.'

'And if you're mistaken?'

'I'll have to kill you to prove it.'

123

There was the sound of another car on the track, east of the corner and driven fast. Van Ruyden jerked his head and the pistol and for an instant Paul thought of chancing a grab. But the gun came back and van Ruyden said:

'Wait.'

The car's nose came round the bend and stopped dead. A big man got out, two hundred pounds of him, and two others, much younger, were close behind. He said in a fine western whinny:

'Don't be silly, boy. Put that thing away.'

When James Scobell had telephoned Cyprus it was a woman's voice which had answered him, and now it was ringing back again with news of two people he'd believed were connected. Mrs Shay was in her house as usual being visited by a man called Martiny, but George Amyas had been found dead in a swimming pool and it was the Englishman who'd discovered his body. In the circumstances it seemed wise to keep tabs on him and this was being discreetly done.... Any further instructions?

He'd ring back in an hour.

James Scobell poured four fingers and swallowed two. His first feeling was one of simple relief: something of menace was happening in Cyprus but it wasn't the danger he'd feared most of all, some amateur in the world of Intelligence. Killing a man like Amyas was outside the ambit of amateur spying, so whatever the problem it wasn't that. What it was he preferred not to guess; he must see. He knew little but that little alarmed him. Peter van Ruyden had flown to Athens and there he had promptly disappeared; Peter van Ruyden was old Julius's grandson.

Scobell picked a New York newspaper from a pile which he had put aside, turning again to a paragraph which

124

when he'd first read it had meant very little. It was a paragraph in the financial pages and it was carefully worded, it named no names, but his country had some very strange laws which allowed you to be as rich as Croesus provided you didn't attempt to fix prices. Scobell considered them mostly useless. There were good arguments for destroying capitalism and at times James Scobell had come close to believing them, but if you accepted the beast you accepted its nature and its nature was to defend itself by any and every means apparent.

Like the van Ruydens, for instance, he thought uneasily, a family which would fight back fiercely against any attempt to fence its pastures. James Scobell had never heard the quotation but had formed settled and somewhat sombre conclusions about the nature of the human animal, and what had happened in Cyprus had a familiar smell, the unmistakable odour of naked power politics.

And Americans were clearly involved, which was something much worse than merely ominous. After fifteen years of work in England James Scobell saw his principal duty precisely. It was to protect his alarming countrymen from the troubles they made for themselves abroad and in the process for James Scobell himself whose whole value depended on trust by Englishmen.

Nevertheless he hesitated. If all this went back to old Julius van Ruyden to take a hand in the game could be more than perilous. Playing poker with very rich men *was* perilous. You thought the stakes had been fixed but very often they hadn't. They could be something very different indeed from what you believed you were playing for.

But finally he returned to the telephone.... The watch on Paul Martiny was sensible and there was another matter, a man called van Ruyden. It was possible he'd
125

slipped into the country, in which case he'd probably gone into hiding. James Scobell would like him located at once. He was an American and his head was bandaged. Meanwhile he would catch the first plane himself.

He'd been talking again in fluent Turkish and as he put the receiver down he smiled. It would be pleasant to see his wife again, it had been almost two months since he last had done so.

Only three of the men who employed Scobell were aware that their man in London was married. There'd been another wife once but that had ended, an American who had coldly divorced him. So only three men knew he'd married again and only one of these three knew the lady's name. She had made Scobell extremely happy but he'd never brought her to London or even wished to. He had left her where she'd been born and was happy. She was thirty years younger and wholly charming, the marriage had been an immense success. The accident she was a Turk was irrelevant.

'Don't be silly, boy. Put that thing away.'

Van Ruyden swung the gun on Scobell who had stopped and removed his cigar to utter. 'Let me tell you how I see this affair.' His manner was entirely reasonable, he was discussing a business proposition. 'I can tell by the way you hold a gun that it isn't a weapon you often use. Naturally that won't stop you killing me—at this range you can hardly miss twice. But you're not good enough or fast enough to hit me and both of my friends in a burst. One or both of them will get to you and if I'm dead they'll be very rough indeed. I happen to be their brother-in-law.

The two Turks had moved level with James Scobell, standing unmoving, watching intently. Greeks would have fidgeted, talked or smoked, but these dark-skinned young

126

men had a saurian calm. 'Next move to you,' James Scobell said pleasantly.

'What are *you* going to do? I have the gun.'

'To begin with I'm going to do the honours.' He looked at Paul and Judie, bowing. 'This gentleman is called Peter van Ruyden and he's a diplomat in the American service. You, if my information is right, will be Paul Martiny and Mrs Shay. I know that's a clumsy introduction but while that gun is still out it will have to do. My own name is James Scobell, at your service.'

'Delighted,' Paul said. Judie Shay said nothing.

James Scobell returned to Peter van Ruyden. 'You were asking what I intended to do, but one thing I don't is to call the police.' He drew on his cigar reflectively. 'I think I'd do well to be perfectly frank. I know who you are and where you're living, so if I want you I can always reach you. But I'm not at all sure that I do really want you. That's the only hard advantage you have. What I *don't* want is a public embarrassment and until I know more that's a very real risk.'

'What do you know?'

'Quite a lot but not everything. I know what was in your safe since you told me, and I'd guessed that Mrs Shay would have it, or maybe it's Mr Martiny now. Since you've been trying to hold them up with a pistol that guess has been very clearly confirmed. What I don't know is why you want it. I could guess again and I know your background, but with a man like your grandfather it's very dangerous to guess. To act prematurely is suicidal.'

Peter van Ruyden's voice was fading. 'Which takes us?' he said.

'Which takes us for the moment to stalemate. I want to talk to these people and think again. I am giving no

127

guarantee for the future but for the moment you're perfectly free to go.'

'And if I decline?'

Scobell turned his head sideways, said something in Turkish.

For the first time Paul Martiny spoke. 'He's sick and he's taken a drug. He told us.'

'Has he indeed? I thought he'd been drinking.' Scobell looked at Peter van Ruyden hard; he said as a matter of simple fact: 'In a matter of minutes you're going out like a light. That deals me four aces, at least for the moment.'

'I could shoot you first.'

'We discussed shooting before. I had hoped you'd agree it would get you no place. You'd be dead yourself before reaching Martiny.'

Van Ruyden said: 'I——' He was almost gone. James Scobell saw it and waited quietly.

'I——'

He collapsed.

Scobell spoke to the Turks who picked him up, propping him by the abandoned two-stroke. Scobell looked at the wreck of Judie's car. 'We'll send for that and have it brought in.' One of the Turks had taken the pistol. 'Not much point in that, they're quite easy to buy here. Meanwhile I should like to take you home. I suspect there's a matter of mutual interest.'

11

Scobell's house was in Kirlizade Street, almost opposite Haidar Pasha mosque. The façade had stood for over a century but inside he had made it modestly comfortable without losing its essential character, that of an old-fashioned Turkish home, neither grand nor poor but a place to live in. He ushered them through to the inner courtyard, an arched colonnade round three sides of the four. There were a central flower bed and fountain, not playing now, hibiscus bushes, oleanders and zinnias. It was dusty and hot but had a peace almost tangible.

A woman rose from a basket chair to receive them. If she felt surprise she did not show it and James Scobell made the introductions. 'My wife,' he said as he held her hand. Judie Shay noticed he squeezed it fondly. The woman smiled at her guests but her husband first, saying something in Turkish which Scobell translated. 'She doesn't speak a word of English and I've no intention of having her learn it. She asks you to excuse her appearance.'

'Tell her I think she looks perfectly charming.'

Scobell translated again and the woman blushed. She wore trousers and an embroidered housecoat, her black hair was wound in a single plait; she had beautiful teeth and bare feet, unpainted, and the skin of her face and her generous arms was the colour of a high-caste Hindu's. She might have been either side of thirty and she discharged an aura of tranquil happiness as something which was physically sensible.

She bowed to her guests and slipped away, and Scobell said: 'She's gone to make coffee.' He waved them to chairs and sat down himself, taking his tie off, relaxing contentedly. He was very much at his ease, the householder. It was clear that this wasn't his holiday hide-out and far less where he kept his mistress: it was his home, where his heart was and where he would die. In a year or two when they pensioned him off he would live here and give no thought to his country.

'I should apologize,' he said, 'and I do. I mean that I cannot offer you drink.' He held a hand up and smiled. 'No, I haven't turned Muslim. As it happens I'm not a Christian either in any sense the word has meaning, but I was born one and all renegades shock me. But my wife is a Muslim and she's younger than I am. It's pleasant to pay her occasional compliments, so when I'm in her house I don't drink.' He was talking easily, to relax the tension. 'As a matter of fact I don't drink here at all. I could use a hotel without too much offending her, but when I'm working I know I drink far too much, so I use my time here to dry myself out. I don't doubt it does me a deal of good and nothing pleases a proper woman more than the knowledge a man will give something up for her.'

Paul Martiny, as Scobell had intended, was beginning to relax in turn. He was looking round the peaceful courtyard, smiling though he didn't know it. 'I should find it worth while myself,' he said. 'I can see you're a very happy man.'

'I've been unlucky in my time. Now I'm not. But there'll be questions you certainly want to ask me.'

130

'There are a great many things which I don't understand.'

'Of course there are. After coffee, though.'

Two children had come into the courtyard, stopping suddenly at the sight of strangers. The colour of their skin was their mother's and they stood silent with all of a Turk's immobility, not frightened but simply awaiting their cue. Scobell called them in Turkish and they ran over at once, then he said in a slow and careful English: 'These are my friends and this is our house.' The girl made a tiny uncertain curtsey and the boy took Martiny's hand in his own. Then they sat on the ground at Scobell's feet. 'I'm having them taught English, you see. It's the only common language here, and in any case it's useful anywhere. But I've no ambition to change their lives. They're their mother's children as well as mine and I don't believe in meddling with backgrounds, nor that my own way of life is much better than theirs.'

Scobell's wife came back with an old brass tray and they drank the thick sweet coffee comfortably. When they had finished she smiled and left them, taking the two children with her. She didn't need a word of English to sense that her husband wished to talk.

Scobell offered Paul a large cigar. 'It's very natural if you want to ask questions but maybe I could save some time if I answered a few without the asking. There were some names named when that man held you up and I told you my own was James Scobell. But I ought to go rather further than that.' He blew smoke at the blazing sky above them. 'I work for a certain organization which not every man in the world approves of.' He named it matter-of-factly, not with pride but equally not with shame. 'That has nothing to do with my life down here, but I'm married to a Turk and I like them. When I can I do rather more

131

than like them. When the Greeks get more than usually bloody there are things I can sometimes do and I do them. I don't meddle in the local politics, or not in any general way, but I interest myself in the grosser injustices and sometimes I manage to have them lessened. So I have Turkish connections who will often oblige me. That's why I came on the scene today, or rather it's how I had the knowledge that you might be in a serious danger. Frankly, I asked friends to shadow you. That man van Ruyden's my major interest, but I'd a very good reason, not born in this island, to believe that van Ruyden had an interest in *you*. Or perhaps in Mrs Shay, or in both of you. And if that were right it could be a violent interest. So when I heard that both of you were motoring on a lonely road I went after you and I'd guessed it right.'

'We're grateful,' Paul said, 'but we're still in the dark.'

'Naturally—that was only the how. For the why we must go back to London, where van Ruyden, who's a proper diplomat, not an agent with diplomatic cover, bribed an official called Amyas, a man in Security, to give him what I must call a paper. As Intelligence in my professional sense this paper was completely useless, but buying it from an English official had complications which I needn't recite. These multiplied a hundredfold when van Ruyden, who had the paper, was burgled. The thief took the fifty thousand pounds which was apparently George Amyas's price but he also took the paper too.'

There was a long silence till Paul Martiny said: 'And Amyas has been found here murdered.'

'After calling on Mrs Shay.'

'You know that?'

'I told you that I had friends. Call them leg-men.'

'And why do you think he called on her?'

Scobell didn't answer but rose from his chair. 'If I were

in your position, sir, I should wish to talk to Mrs Shay.'
He began to walk away but she stopped him. She said
to Paul:

'We'll have to play. He knows more than enough to
guess the rest.'

James Scobell turned and bowed politely. 'I'm grateful—
you're making it very much easier.' Paul's cigar had gone
out and he gave him another. 'Then on the basis that
we've a mutual interest, and I emphasize I'm no sort of
policeman, it was Mrs Shay's husband who blew that safe.
Where the money is I do not care but I care about that
paper intensely.' He looked at them, friendly but deadly
serious. 'One or other of you,' he said, 'must have it.'

'We'll proceed on the assumption, then, that one of us
must have this paper.'

'It's rather better than an assumption, you know. I told
you I had useful friends and one saw van Ruyden leave
your room yesterday. Since he tried to hold you up this
morning it's certain he didn't get what he wanted.'

'I caught him but had no idea who he was. I thought he
was a local poor white, some wretch on his uppers. I let him
go.'

'Unfortunate.'

'As you tell it, very.' Paul reflected some time. 'Did van
Ruyden kill George Amyas, then?'

'I would bet on it.'

'But why does a diplomat do a murder?'

'He didn't murder as a diplomat. When that paper fell
into other hands Amyas had to get it back, and if he had
he'd have certainly broken his bargain. With van Ruyden,
who would never have seen what his money had been
intended to pay for. George Amyas wanted his paper back
but he'd never have dared to hand it over—not after somebody else had seen it. Van Ruyden had worked that out for

133

himself and he wanted that paper extremely badly. Now Amyas was his rival. He killed him.'

There was a silence again while Paul thought it over. The children came back with soft drinks on the tray, solemn-eyed and polite and moving softly. From the house there was the smell of cooking. 'Lunch,' Scobell said. 'I hope you'll stay. Turkish cooking can be rather nasty but properly done it can also be good. It's the rice which really makes it or breaks it. When that's done well it's often delicious.'

Paul had reached a decision he couldn't avoid. 'I have that paper,' he said, 'and I've read it. What puzzles me is that you said it was useless.'

'As Intelligence it's entirely pointless but that doesn't mean that it couldn't be used. Look at the name at the bottom. That's dynamite.'

'Then van Ruyden was going to use it. How?'

'I don't know that, or not in detail, but any guesses I make all point one way. The van Ruydens were going to use it politically—I mean in our own domestic politics.' Scobell stared at Paul. 'Does that name ring a bell?'

'Even to an Englishman—yes.'

'Then apart from the pleasure of seeing my wife that's the reason I've been taking an interest. You mustn't mis-understand me, though. I've no moral feelings how tycoons run their empires but I'm a professional in Intelligence and I happen to be based in England. My work depends largely on mutual trust and it was an American who bribed George Amyas. If that were discovered, as some time it would be, I'd lose most of fifteen years of work. So I'll make you a proposition.'

'Shoot.'

'Give me that paper. I mean to destroy it.'

'We could destroy it ourselves.'

134

'You'd be wasting an asset.' Scobell who'd been lolling at ease sat up sharply. 'I told you that I worked in Intelligence, which means that I have some unusual contacts.' Now he was looking at Judie Shay. 'Your husband's in prison doing an eighter.'

'You're not offering to have him sprung?' She knew what sort of life would follow and it wasn't one which she wished to live.

'Nothing so plain damned silly as that. But if I'm not misinformed he's a model prisoner and I've a friend who is very influential indeed. He'd be every bit as upset as I am to know that that paper you hold existed, but he'd also be a delighted man to know that I was going to destroy it and he's in a position to pay any debt he would owe me. Mrs Shay, I will make you a modest bet. I will lay you one hundred pounds to five that the moment your husband comes up for parole he will get it as a matter of course.'

Judie was sitting rigid, thinking. She knew enough of the world Paul Martiny moved in to realize Scobell would not be boasting. Who rose and said: 'I'll give a hand with the lunch,' and this time she didn't stop him leaving.

Judie turned to Paul but he shook his head. 'Your property,' he said. 'Your decision.'

'But how do you see it?'

'As a very fair gamble. He could do what he says, I don't doubt that. He'd work in the shadows of course, but it's on. He'll go to his friend who'll be high in Security and the friend would be very much more than relieved to know that this time bomb had now been defused. Scobell could ask a price and he'd get it. A word here, a hint there —that's how that world works.'

'And Scobell's own motive for playing ball?'

'I know nothing about high Security, but when he says that it works on an old boy network I'm prepared to be-

135

lieve that he's telling the truth. In that case he'll be inside the net but he'd be out on his ear if events broke wrong for him. He's an American and so is van Ruyden. I don't follow the situation in detail, to do that I should have to know things I don't, but I can see that what van Ruyden did could be disastrous for James Scobell.' Paul nodded decidedly. 'Yes, there's a motive.'

'We could also destroy the thing ourselves.'

'That's what we'll certainly have to do if we don't accept this proposition. To us this is useless, a standing danger. If we kept it we could do nothing with it. Jack isn't a blackmailer. Nor am I.'

'You're saying we're on to something for nothing?'

'Life never gives that but I'd put it like this. If Scobell should mean to double cross us I can't conceive what the double cross is, and if he doesn't we're getting a pretty good price for something which to us is a nuisance.'

'I'd like to have Jack back.'

'I know.' If it sounded flat he hadn't intended it, but he knew perfectly where he stood with Judie.

Scobell came back with news of lunch and as they ate he made the conversation, talking easily in English and Turkish. He said something to his wife in the latter and she nodded and smiled, very clearly flattered. In English he said: 'It's very odd. I've read somewhere that if you want to live happily with a woman who doesn't speak your language the essential is never to learn to speak hers. I haven't found that true in practice, and anyway it wouldn't have worked. I told you I don't interfere with politics—they'd deport me at once if I started that—but I do know a great many Turks and I like them. They come to me with little things and I do what I can as elderly uncle.'

'The Greeks treat them badly?'

136

'That's politics. Careful. Just say there are roughly four Greeks to one Turk and a collection of broken-down foreign soldiery who'd be useless in any serious trouble. All serious trouble starts from some trifle, so if I can sometimes smooth one down I don't feel I'm wholly wasting my time. If I'm a thorn in certain gentlemen's flesh that's something I can bear quite bravely.'

Judie said softly to Paul: 'I'll trust him.'

'I think you've made the right decision.'

In the car after lunch he gave her the envelope and she handed it to Scobell through the window. 'Thank you for lunch,' she said. 'Good hunting.'

'It's been a pleasure. Until we meet again. I'll be flying back to England on Monday but there isn't a reason to shorten your visit. If you're thinking about van Ruyden forget him.'

'You live an interesting life,' Paul Martiny said.

'I'm afraid you're very much mistaken. Ninety-nine per cent is just office routine.'

'And the one per cent?'

'That works mostly on hunches.'

The car took the pair of them back to Kyrenia, dropping Paul first at the hotel door. 'Dinner tonight?' he asked.

'Not tonight. It's been the hell of a day and I want to think.'

'Very well,' he said. He was not astonished. After all she had a husband in prison and they'd been discussing how to get him out. He wasn't her husband and never would be.

Judie went back to her flat to rest. It was the hottest part of the afternoon but she hated all forms of air conditioning. She wrapped a sheet round her stomach and turned on a fan; she lay down but for once she didn't sleep. Her mind was in two separate tensions, disappoint-

137

ment and relief competing. The disappointment was for her affair with Paul which had suddenly, unexpectedly soured. It was no good pretending it hadn't gone wrong. She had taken him for what he could give her, that he heightened her consciousness, brought her alive, but what he'd laid on her doorstep, though unintending, had been a murder, a hold-up, idiot violence, strange discussion with a stranger American who moved in a world she instinctively hated. You couldn't play light opera against a background of the noises of battle. It was futile to try so she wrote it off.

She wrote it off reluctantly and turned to the very real relief. If that American had meant what he said she'd have her husband out before they broke him, and this time they'd have done just that. There'd been a letter from Jack Shay that morning, cheerful and uncomplaining as ever. He had always been a model prisoner but she knew that he never settled to prison. Some men could somehow suspend their lives but Jack had never learnt to do that. He'd earn his remission but that wasn't enough. But with parole she might get him back as he had been, something recognizable as the man she had married.

... That paper he had unwittingly stolen. Paul Martiny. Mr James Scobell. The kaleidoscope had shaken its pattern. She'd betrayed Jack Shay but in a sense she had saved him. Illogical? Of course it was. What woman would care for the dialectic? Only one thing was presently certain: she couldn't go on with Paul Martiny. Somehow, though this was totally senseless, somehow it was all Paul's fault.

James Scobell was also trying to sleep and he too was finding the goddess fickle. He had spoken to Paul Martiny of hunches and it was a hunch which was keeping him tossing restlessly. In theory the affair had been settled and Scobell began to tick off the plusses. He hadn't a doubt he

138

could do as he'd promised, he knew just the man to approach to do it, retired by now, an *éminence grise*, but a man who could talk to any Minister and be listened to with much more than respect. Perhaps it wasn't guaranteed but then he hadn't offered one; he'd offered twenty to one in five-pound notes and he considered those were conservative odds. And whatever happened he'd still have the paper, his fifteen years of hard graft preserved. George Amyas had been neutralized—dead. Peter van Ruyden had probably killed him.

Probably—that was very relevant. James Scobell had no shadow of proof to embarrass him and nobody else would suspect he had. That was more than merely relevant, it was very important to James Scobell. A man like that Angelides could make things very awkward indeed if he suspected Scobell of withholding evidence. Scobell knew him, disliked him, but also respected, for they'd had several brushes, one quite notable, when Scobell had contrived to bring to nothing some plan which Angelides's master set store on. All these plans had involved bad news for a Turk. Asterios Angelides would be delighted to see James Scobell's broad back but so far he'd walked his tightrope successfully.

He rolled his two hundred pounds over fretfully; he was troubled but couldn't pin it down. Peter van Ruyden presented no problem. Like Amyas he'd been successfully neutralized, not by death but by normal provident action. Scobell knew where he lived and could always reach him.

Martiny and Judie Shay were guarded. Van Ruyden was that rarest of problems, the sort which, ignored, just went quietly away. Literally went away since van Ruyden could do nothing else. Evidently he was very sick, and if he was taking the drug which Scobell suspected it was a question

139

of days till he broke down finally. Scobell could fly back to London happily.

Nevertheless he tossed and sweated. It wasn't reasonable but still he worried. Like Judie he mistrusted logic, though for reasons which were very different. Judie Shay was an attractive woman with a proper contempt for all masculine thinking, but Scobell had a long and deep experience and when his thumbs pricked he'd learnt to heed the message.

There was something to come still, something unpleasant.

12

Asterios Angelides was a man with a healthy contempt for clichés, and phrases like keeping your options open simply struck him as a circumlocution for saying you would do nothing whatever until circumstances forced some reluctant action. But prudence was entirely different, especially in something like Amyas's death which he strongly suspected involved a world which every good policeman both feared and hated. Moreover he had known what would happen: one couldn't have British visitors murdered nor escape from the awkward fact of a killing by shrugging it off as the work of shadows from another and very different life where a killing was part of accepted rules for which you as a policeman were not accountable. Angelides had known all this but had decided to let the situation develop. There would be pressures but he'd decided to bear them. All this was sound, a trained policeman's thinking. Unhappily he had misjudged the timing.

For he'd been sent for and it had not gone well. The man in black was out of the country, appearing at an organization which existed for the dubious purpose of giving to him and to others like him the illusion that their States were important. The summons had not offended him, though he would certainly have considered it insult if he'd been called before some stooge civilian, what was laughingly still called a Minister. These came and went in circumstances which were sometimes obscure and often suspect and nobody paid them the least attention. So he hadn't felt humiliated to be asked to attend by a man of power, a representative of those other men who in matters of any real importance ran the country with astonishing competence.

The chaplain sat Angelides down. Both of them were essentially Greek, which meant an appearance of total frankness, at any rate in the opening gambits. What would develop later on might be something very different indeed. The chaplain said:

'This man George Amyas and his unfortunate death. It's really very troublesome.'

'I realize that as well as you do.'

'Not quite as well as me, I think. The British High Commissioner has presented a rather formal letter.'

'Wasn't that inevitable?'

'Yes. You mustn't misunderstand me, though.' The chaplain held a hand up and smiled. 'Her Majesty's Commissioner here holds a position of no weight or influence. Since in private life he's also sensible he knows this just as well as we do and he only writes us formal letters on instructions from his masters in London. So how shall I put it? They want reassurance.'

'And if they don't get it?'

'There's the rub. In any normal circumstances the British could do nothing effective. I know there are certain financial arrangements and it would be sensible to use them as levers. But the British will never do that—they daren't. The liberal Left would be round their ears, to say nothing of the romantic Right which believes the word Commonwealth still has meaning. But that new mining

142

concession is something different. We stand to make a good deal of money and for the moment only London is interested. You follow me? I'm sure you do. A word here, a nod there, and the business goes cold. That would never come out in Parliament but that's how the City of London works.' The chaplain leant forward. 'You know what George Amyas was?'

'Of course.'

'Then one or two thoughts occur to me. His body had been robbed, I believe.'

Asterios Angelides nodded.

'My advice would be to forget the fact.' The chaplain smiled, one Greek to another. 'I realize there must be certain temptations, but some impoverished Turk found with Amyas's watch will not, in the circumstances, end our embarrassment.'

'Not credible?'

'Too coincidental.'

'You want me to find the real killer, then?'

The chaplain said blandly: 'I didn't say that.'

'Just as well since he's probably left the country.'

'I see that you understand me perfectly.' The chaplain rose and shook hands warmly. 'Good fortune,' he said. 'Report back to me, please.'

Mr Angel went back to his office to think, realizing that what he'd been handed was in effect the politest of ultimata. He began to think about Paul Martiny whom he'd once, almost idly, considered framing. Under pressure the thought had both substance and urgency, and it wasn't quite inconceivable that it might only be a framing in name. Inevitably any evidence would be something which he would have to arrange but it wasn't beyond credibility's limits that Paul Martiny knew who had killed George Amyas. Angelides was a good official and like all good

143

officials liked to see it on paper. He wrote in idiomatic Greek:

1. *There is an established connection between George Amyas and the woman Shay. He is known to have called on her before he was killed. Mrs Shay's husband is one sort of criminal, and from a police point of view George Amyas was another. There is a curiosity here but nothing incredible.*

2. *There is equally an admitted connection between the woman and Mr Paul Martiny. He has admitted to spending the night with her. He is probably her protector as well as her lover.*

3. *Martiny finds Amyas dead in the pool in circumstances which, taken alone, impute no suspicion to Paul Martiny. But I see little good reason to take them alone.*

Angelides read this through with distaste. These were facts but they did little to help him. The square could be closed on the fourth of its sides by accepting the very simple assumption that whatever it was which bound the Shays and Amyas had also brought Paul Martiny to Cyprus, but Angelides was an experienced policeman who'd been trained to look for motive first, and some interest in common, if indeed it existed, was a long way short of a motive for murder. No doubt there were plenty of men who had one, for Amyas must have made many enemies and some of these would be fellow professionals with the means as well as the will to kill. But Martiny hadn't the smell of a killer, and if he were rather a special kind, a man whose own air was his primary cover, he was behaving very oddly indeed. No one with motive to murder Amyas

144

would use other than a professional killer and no pro would hang round after earning his money for no better reason than bedding a woman.

Angelides frowned for that wasn't now accurate. Bedding a woman? It seemed he had ceased to. Angelides had had no trouble in bugging Judie Shay's apartment—the maid was the wife of a senior sergeant—but the bug had brought nothing of any interest for the good and wholly sufficient reason that Martiny hadn't gone there again. This was confirmed from more positive sources, the men he had ordered to watch the house. Mrs Shay and Mr Paul Martiny had had dinner together the previous evening, but they had done so at Martiny's hotel and the informant's report on that had been negative. They'd been polite and appeared to be perfectly friendly but they hadn't had the air of lovers. That had happened before and would happen again, the affair which flared up and died down as quickly, but Martiny would be an experienced man and he wouldn't fight on on hopeless ground, especially if it were also ground where he happened to have committed a murder.

To an intelligent Hellene such an action made nonsense but he realized that none of the actors was Greek. He sat and smoked moodily, seeing no answer, and when the telephone broke the rat-race of thought he welcomed the relief of action. It was his informant in Paul Martiny's hotel and Martiny had cancelled his reservation. He had booked on the regular flight next day.

Angelides bit his lip in frustration. If this man left the island he'd lose his lead, the only path to the truth which looked even hopeful. He still didn't believe that Paul was a killer, he might even not know the killer's name, but an instinct was insisting increasingly that if he didn't himself possess a motive he knew what it was and perhaps who

145

held it. Angelides was severely tempted. He could pull in Martiny and have him, well, questioned. His country's representatives would reluctantly come to his aid in the end but they hadn't earned the reputation that they crusaded in their nationals' interests and Angelides could feel confident of a night and a day to break Paul Martiny. He mustn't burn him no doubt or otherwise mark him but nowadays there were other methods. He hadn't learnt them on his police course in England.

He shook his head—it was too big a gamble. If he pulled in this man and he didn't talk, if his instinct was wrong and he *couldn't* talk, then Asterios Angelides would be thrown to the wolves without a tremor, not at the urging of British officials whose protests would be shrugged away but simply as a policeman who'd failed. Overplaying a hand was the one sin fatal.

He sent for an airline timetable: the flight for London tomorrow left after lunch. That gave him a night to sleep on it, and experience had taught him firmly that when things started moving they moved again. Judie Shay's house was bugged and covered, he had an eye in Paul Martiny's hotel. Who was leaving tomorrow, he hadn't much time. Time for what? Let time itself resolve the question. When things started moving ...

They moved at eleven o'clock precisely, eleven that evening and almost cool. The telephone woke Angelides roughly and an excited Inspector began to gabble.

'Control yourself. The facts, please. Shortly.'

They were alarming enough but to Angel decisive. The man watching Judie's house had been shot. He had a hole in his stomach and would probably die. He was in hospital and still unconscious, but before they had put him out to operate he'd said something about a foreigner who'd tried to force his way into the house he was guarding.

146

Asterios Angelides let his breath out in a contented sigh. The gods had been kind and he accepted it gratefully.

'Arrest Mr Paul Martiny. Break him. I will give you until midnight tomorrow.'

Peter van Ruyden was trying to think normally, something he found increasingly difficult as the pain and the unknown drug destroyed him. Two failures had greatly decreased his chances, and the second, on the corniche road, had been a failure of an ominous kind. James Scobell must have taken a hand in the game, he could hardly have appeared by coincidence, and any interest by a man like Scobell could only be an interest which ran sharply against van Ruyden's own. Why he had cut himself in was a guess but he worked for a powerful organization and a whisper in van Ruyden's country would be more than enough to put it in gear. Or Scobell, who knew the start of the story, could have reported it and been ordered to act.

Van Ruyden, when he wasn't drugged, had a disciplined mind and he fought to use it. It wasn't important to know for certain what hand had put the machine in gear: what mattered was that Scobell was acting and for this he might have one or two motives. It was probable, though not yet proven, that he wanted the Report himself, but even if that wasn't the case it was evident he had no intention of letting van Ruyden obtain it himself. In either case James Scobell was an enemy and van Ruyden had enough already.

So forget about James Scobell. Take the Shays. Shay stole that Report but can hardly have planned to; he may not have grasped its potential politically. But certainly Paul Martiny will have and Martiny is Mrs Shay's protector. To the Shays it has only one value—blackmail. It's natural

147

that the man holds the paper but the woman will have the final say. After all, it belongs to her, not Martiny. It would have been simpler and a great deal quicker if I could have had it from the man directly, but I must face the fact that as things have broken there is little chance left of that, or none. Then I must go to the woman and change the weapons. The only one left is money. I have it.

He waited until ten o'clock, then took the motorbike out of the shed where he kept it, enjoying the cooling evening air as he rode it across the pass to Kyrenia. The Turks on their roadblock waved a greeting; they knew his bandaged head by now and in any case he wasn't a Greek. He even knew how to make them laugh, which was to stop and look solemn, say: 'I'm no Greek.'

He propped the bike against Judie's garden wall, walking up the short drive openly. He'd made more than one recce and knew the lay-out, an old stone-built house in its fashion still elegant, creeper clad and with an untidy garden. Van Ruyden approved of Judie's taste—this was pleasanter than some concrete box. The old house was now two separate flats and Judie had the upper one. A separate staircase had been built on outside.

He had his foot on the first of the steps to climb them when a hand came down on his shoulder hard. Its owner spun him rudely and stared.

Van Ruyden stared back, at a loss and showing it. He had expected that the house would be watched, maybe by one of Scobell's young Turks, but he hadn't expected a uniformed policeman. The man stood there stolidly, waiting for movement. Van Ruyden could see he was armed. So was he. James Scobell had been right, they were easy to buy. Van Ruyden had had to pay far too much but he'd found another pistol at once.

The last thing he wished was occasion to use it, his

weapon was money now, not violence. He said to the policeman:

'Can you speak English?'

'They obliged me to learn it at school.' No 'Sir'.

'I am calling on Mrs Judie Shay.'

'Nobody calls on Mrs Shay.'

'I don't understand.'

'I have my orders. By day you may call on Mrs Shay provided you have my superiors' clearance. After nine you may not call at all.'

'It's ridiculous,' Peter van Ruyden said.

He knew he had made a mistake at once. In the light at the foot of the stairs the face hardened. The man said something in Cypriot Greek and van Ruyden could understand a good deal of it. None of it was at all polite. He said in good Greek:

'That was very rude.'

The man looked astonished. 'You speak some Greek?'

'I learnt it in Greece and also the customs.' Van Ruyden was on top again, or Peter van Ruyden thought he was. The situation offended his sense of propriety but it was also a very familiar one. This was something which could be resolved by money. He pulled out two five-pound notes and fingered them. 'I told you I'd been in Greece,' he said. 'Certain courtesies are quite acceptable.'

The policeman looked at the notes; he was clearly tempted. 'No,' he said finally. 'No, I dare not.'

Van Ruyden produced another fiver. 'No,' the man said, but much more weakly.

Peter van Ruyden lost his patience. He was prepared to bribe but not to bargain and fifteen pounds was well over the odds.... Three Scotsmen, two Jews, a single Greek. He knew he'd paid far too much for his pistol and he resented being cheated again. Besides, he hadn't the time to chaffer.

149

Fifteen pounds would be nearly a fortnight's net pay. He thrust the fivers into the policeman's belt and started to push an impatient way past him.

The answer was the last he'd expected. If the policeman had drawn his gun and waved it van Ruyden would not have been wholly astonished, but a blow in the Anglo-Saxon manner was something he was unprepared for. He didn't even see it coming and it caught him on his bandaged eye. The agony was immediate; his knees crumpled and he fell untidily. Then he saw the boot moving towards his face and he knew that he couldn't take another.

Peter van Ruyden drew and fired.

Paul Martiny was packing unhappily. Judie had made it clear it was ended, gracefully but sufficiently firmly, and since he was a fair-minded man he couldn't with any honesty blame her. It wasn't for this she had planned to take him—not a lunatic American who used firearms and wanted that wicked Report for a reason which James Scobell was concealing if indeed he really knew what it was. She hadn't contracted for crazy violence, nor the discords of other people's intrigues. So when they had left the Scobells' house she had sent him home without asking him in, and the following evening, after dinner together, she had smiled and had kissed him but ordered a taxi.

It had been cool perhaps, but so was Judie. No one could call her sentimental and he hadn't himself supposed she was. If it came to that he hadn't been cheated since he'd been anything but some lovelorn boy who'd dashed blindly in without counting the cost. On the contrary, Paul Martiny thought wryly, he had counted the cost with a good deal of care. His ideal of an affair with Judie had been a matter of three to six months at most and he'd been anything but blissfully happy in accepting that if she took him at all she would hold him until Jack Shay came out, a steady and almost formal liaison of a kind he had never accepted before. He had wanted her badly enough to do so and equally he had guessed why she'd taken him. So when it had soured she had shut it down. No contract express or implied had been broken. He couldn't blame Judie, they were two of a kind.

A knock interrupted this civilized thinking, disappointment and what was close to relief in a balance he wouldn't have cared to examine. It was the manager, sweating and obviously frightened. 'The police have called again,' he said.

'My friend Mr Angel?'

'Not Mr Angel. Three uniformed men and they're none of them local.'

'I'll come at once.'

'I'd be grateful for your co-operation. They're in the road in a car and they'd like to talk there.'

Paul walked down to the car and a man climbed out. He opened a rear door invitingly. Paul climbed in and the first man joined him smoothly. There was a second on his other side. The driver let in the clutch and they moved away.

In the car they were gentle enough in manner but in a windowless room they were notably less so. Very soon they were being quite other than gentle.

13

When James Scobell learnt of Paul's arrest, as he learnt of everything else which concerned him, he broke the rule which he had boasted of and went out to a hotel bar for a drink. It was one which was used by journalists and he needed the whisky much less than the talk. He knew that he must make a decision and he suspected that long established habit, the life he had made for himself in the island, had blunted the fine edge of judgement. Another intelligent man's was essential.

He found what he wanted and bought him a drink, not an old old hand with Scobell's own tolerance nor a newcomer drugged with outrageous publicity. But this man had been in Cyprus long enough to be discovering the real position.... The tourists went to the tourists' resorts where there wasn't the least sign of trouble; they sat in the sun but they sat on a bomb. No country on earth was quite so uneasy nor under its shining skin so explosive. Not including the British who would stay in their bases, seven bodies of armed men infested it—eight if you counted assorted hirelings who played at soldiering under nobody's flag, something no local realist did. And the arms in private hands were uncountable. A spark could send it all up in a minute, and the simple but inescapable fact, known to all Greeks but never mentioned, was that Turkey was very much nearer than Greece. No wonder the country was run rather oddly.

James Scobell knew all this but was glad to hear it. In a crisis a man must be sure of the background and he realized Martiny's arrest was a crisis. He had told him that Angelides would be delighted to see his own broad back, but he had always been entirely scrupulous, always James Scobell, a private citizen, never talking of his organization nor hinting at the huge power behind him. He had married a Turk and was therefore suspect, but it was suspicion of James Scobell the man, a tiresome but also resourceful nuisance who would sometimes frustrate the more grievous injustices.

All that could change in a day and would. It would if Mr Angel found out that Martiny had visited Scobell's house. He had taken him there without hesitation since in the area where Scobell roosted Angelides's writ simply did not run. His house wasn't watched—it couldn't be watched; his comings and goings were all his own. But Martiny might mention the visit innocently, or more likely under wicked pressure. Mr James Scobell had no illusions what local interrogation could mean.

When Angelides would see the light, it would all be as clear as gin and water, a beverage James Scobell detested. In point of fact he would have it wrong but his conclusion would be far from illogical. George Amyas's job would be known, as Scobell's was too though he never invoked it. But they were the same kinds of work and could well be competing, and George Amyas had been picked up murdered. A visitor called Martiny finds him and shortly after he's calling on James Scobell. What policeman could resist the obvious, especially after another killing, a constable watching the only house where Amyas had had an established contact? Any murder was an unpleasant business and in one way this country was the same as all others: killing a policeman was deadly serious. Anyone even suspect was finished and that would include Scobell himself.

James Scobell went home but still quite sober, for a major decision hung over his head. Angelides, who hated him, had managed to force his hand at last, though it was as certain as anything humanly could be that he hadn't planned it that way nor even foreseen it. But when the pennies from heaven fell down he'd seize them. James Scobell must act first or Scobell was in trouble. Very big trouble indeed. And his family.

Moreover it went against the grain to leave Martiny to the local mercies. Scobell had made him no kind of promise, simply given an undertaking to Judie that he'd use that Report in her husband's interest. But he'd liked Paul Martiny, he had guessed what he did, and if that guess were only a quarter right then the two of them had a hobby in common. Martiny protected criminals, a matter wide open to more than one judgement, but James Scobell protected Turks, and locally that was much worse than crime. So both of them were protectors and suspect. James Scobell, he decided, had a duty of decency. If anyone caught up with Martiny then let it be the British police, let them nail him for what he had really done, not see him framed here for two murders he hadn't. That was the danger now, not van Ruyden. The van Ruydens could be ignored and forgotten since their plans, whatever they'd been, were finished. They weren't the enemies now so write them off. The enemy was Angelides and there was only one way to disarm him. Run. And of course take Paul with you and Judie Shay. It was unthinkable to leave her to pick up the bill.

It would be a wrench for he had grown healthy roots, he'd been happy here and sometimes useful. But he hadn't in practice another choice. Even if they did nothing worse, and Angelides would surely try to, they could deport him by signing a single paper and there wasn't an effective appeal. He might not get his family out or only after years of pressure. Sticking it wasn't a real alternative. What had that journalist said? Enough.

He began to consider the means dispassionately. He would lose his house and he'd grown to love it, but he had a pension shortly due to him and modest means of his own which he'd been saving for years. He'd simply buy another home. Turkey would not be alien to a woman who spoke no other tongue, and as for himself he spoke it fluently. A shock no doubt—she wouldn't like it. What woman would? But she'd know her duty. Also, he sometimes dared to think, she was foolish enough to love James Scobell. He had connections in Turkey and would certainly use them. As for the children Turkey was bigger, and they wouldn't be in a despised minority.

Decision once taken he swung smoothly to action. He had a cabin cruiser in Kyrenia harbour: she was to be victualled and watered and made ready for sea. He talked to two Turks he'd befriended and trusted, then sent for his two brothers-in-law. He was going to need their services in a matter which was distinctly illegal, so they could come with him too if they wished. They had grinned. They could always disappear for a bit and had the protection of their own community. It was different for James Scobell. They'd stay.

Then timing was going to be very important. Martiny wouldn't be held at headquarters but at that villa they used outside the town. It was quieter there and quiet was essential. They had picked him up the previous evening

155

which meant that they'd had him a night and a day. He might have broken by now or perhaps he hadn't, but they could make him say almost anything once they got him on the run at all. So midnight tonight was the deadline—the latest. The *Yellowstone* would be ready, fuelled, and his wife and the children would be going there separately. So was another but English lady, the Mrs Shay they had met on another occasion. That had all been arranged through mutual friends and they needn't give a thought to that side of it. He intended to sail at one o'clock, which gave them an hour to complete their own job and get down to the harbour if nothing went wrong. James Scobell did not intend that it should. So be here at eleven sharp. No knives or guns but clubs if you must.

And some pieces of rope and your prayers for us all.

Paul was exhausted but not quite broken. The worst had been the uncertainty. This country had been under British rule so presumably its police procedure would still have some roots in British practice. Presumably, but it wasn't certain, and as the hours dragged by it seemed less and less likely. They had left him his watch and he looked at it dourly. They had arrested him the previous evening and the time had been just after eleven; it was now nearly midnight the following day which was over the twenty-four hours of licence which he thought he remembered were allowed for 'inquiries'.

They hadn't been hours which he'd care to remember. He hadn't been tortured and the blows had been bearable, delivered more in frustrated anger than as part of the campaign to break him, but every other technique had been ruthlessly used. He had asked to see a lawyer—they'd found one. The man had been a local Greek, his command of English much less than perfect, and after a bit he had slipped away. Paul had asked to speak to the High Commission and had been told it had been informed already. The High Commission no doubt had duties but it also knew its powers precisely. What these were had never been stated clearly, nor those of the men who were trying to break him.

So the uncertainty had been hardest of all, the fear that there wasn't a recognized time limit which must end this interrogation finally. They had kept him standing for sixteen hours, he'd had nothing to eat and the minimal water, there'd been screams from a neighbouring room, cries for mercy, and once they'd opened the door deliberately to show him a man carried past on a stretcher.... Why had he killed the man George Amyas, what were his motives and who were his contacts here? How did Mrs Shay connect and why had he gone to her house that night? Why had he brutally killed a policeman who'd been doing his duty and nothing more? Where had he hidden the weapon? Talk. Talk or it will go very hard. Harder than this. Oh yes, much harder.

He had stood there and grimly told the truth, his physical exhaustion increasing. They had gone at him in teams of two, two men for two hours, then two others, quite fresh. There'd been the light in his eyes to blind him mercilessly, the stifling heat and the lack of water, barely enough to keep him conscious. He knew he was no sort of hero, only a very stubborn man. In any serious pain he'd break down at once; he would say what they wanted, what was more he would sign it. But short of straight torture he could hold for a little.

... I'll be damned if I'll let some Cypriot crack me.

Now he was in another room, on a bench without mattress, unshaven and stinking. The light was still on but the switch was outside, the window was barred and he couldn't

157

open it, the heat in the airless cell was unbearable. In twenty-four hours he'd drunk maybe a pint and his savage thirst was increasing pitilessly. Paul ached for sleep but was not allowed to, even if thirst had made it possible. There was a spyhole in the metal door and ten times in the hour, to the minute precisely, a guard would open it and shake a rattle. And he knew they'd be coming back. They had said so. It was only a question of time and they'd break him.

A question of time, then, but also of pride. Already he wasn't thinking too clearly ... Matilda, his wife—she was half a German. Worse things had happened in Germany. Much. And very much worse in another place, but of course there was the double standard. You killed and killed, maybe millions of men, but provided the intellectuals admired you ...

He pulled himself together sharply. This wouldn't do: he had heard of the symptoms. There was something called dissociation and a competent interrogator would do most things to induce that state. In it you thought strange thoughts, talked wildly. The strange thoughts had begun to arrive, so steady.

He climbed down from the bunk, rather scared that he staggered, and began to walk the cell unsteadily, three steps to the window, three back to the door. As he reached it on the third or fourth turn the spyhole swung open, the face looked in. The guard grunted and banged the spyhole shut.

... It was stupid to let him see me moving. They'll only come back the sooner. Hell.

Paul went back to the bunk and listened tensely, and presently he heard the movement. But it wasn't the sound he'd expected and feared, the confident ring of leathershod feet. Instead there was a strangled cry, then a slither

158

against the door. A bump. The spyhole swung open and a new face appeared at it. A voice said in a fine western whinny:

'Are you alive there?'

'Just about.'

'Hold on a bit while I open the door. Lucky this clown had the key. I'll use it.'

The door opened and James Scobell came in. He had a cosh in one hand, a thermos flask in the other. 'Water,' he said. 'I know the form.'

Martiny drank while Scobell watched him, then Scobell produced two tablets. 'Glucose.' He was as calm as though he'd been hoeing corn. 'We'll have to walk a bit to reach the car.' He permitted himself a social smile. 'I should have explained that we've come to rescue you. It's a melodramatic word, I dare say, but you must remember I wasn't born in England.' He was chatting to give Paul time to collect himself. 'Could you walk a few yards?'

'I could try.'

'Let's go.'

14

They went into the corridor and Martiny saw the guard slumped on the floor. James Scobell bent down and took his pistol. 'I've a bit of a thing against carrying firearms but we haven't the time to truss him up and I don't want to chance his coming to and shooting us in the back as we leave. The other four are out of action—you'll see as we go past their room.' He looked at Paul Martiny doubtfully —he was shakier than he'd first supposed. Scobell knew too much of the local methods to have supposed that he'd find him in vigorous health, but he was leaning against the wall and panting, evidently very close to collapse. Scobell took an arm and began to walk him.

They went past a room with an open door, and as Paul staggered again Scobell waited outside it. Four men were inside, gagged and bound to chairs, their belts hanging from pegs on the wall behind them. James Scobell laughed. 'That was rather silly. If you must carry weapons you should carry them always, not sit down to play cards with your guns out of reach. These four were very easy meat for my brothers-in-law whom you've met before. We came over the wall, then an unlocked door, a couple of coshes and here we are. I took the man outside your cell myself.'

He was matter-of-fact but was secretly worried for he'd

realized he'd have to change his plan. They'd come over the wall as he'd said they had, but it hadn't been quite as simple as that. The wall itself had been less than formidable for active men with a strong rope ladder, but at the top there had been a deep cheval de frise, and though they'd known of it and brought sacks and bolsters it had slowed them since they had had to be careful. For a man who at best was three-quarters conscious a slip would be a serious matter. So the wall wasn't on, they must think again. Scobell frowned—this meant a change of plan. He had hoped to get away unseen, for a start of maybe twenty minutes till the guard on the cell recovered consciousness or one of the others worked free from his bonds. His car was beyond the wall where he'd hidden it, but he knew now that he couldn't reach it. Not over that wall with Paul Martiny.

They stumbled to the end of the corridor and two young men appeared from the shadows. They were all in an open but roofed verandah. Scobell began to talk fast in Turkish and one of them answered, it seemed in protest.

'It's a risk, you know.'

'Of course it's a risk. But we'll never get this one across that wall. If he spikes himself we've all of us had it.'

'Then what do we do?'

'Go back to the car by the wall as we came, then bring it round to the gate where they've put the guardhouse. Have it turned ready to start at once. Flash your lights when it's set. I'll look after this end.'

'And the man in the gatehouse?'

'Will almost certainly open it. He'll come out to see what's going on.'

'He's probably armed.'

'So were the others. Even so I'd prefer that you didn't kill him. And keep the engine running hard.'

161

Scobell and Paul Martiny waited, Paul in a cane-bottomed chair, almost gone, Scobell with hands clenched on the wooden railing. Presently he heard a car start; he said softly and urgently:

'Paul Martiny.'

Paul didn't answer and Scobell shook him gently. In the cell he'd been holding on by a thread but reaction had pushed him right up to his limit. Finally he said weakly: 'Yes?'

'I want you to listen with very great care. I'm going to get you out of here but it may not be entirely easy. A car's coming and it'll be flashing its lights. When it does we shall have to go to it. Quickly. It's too risky to bring it right up to the house so it'll wait at the gate and we'll have to get there.' James Scobell looked down the gravelled drive. 'Twenty-five yards, I should say. Can you make it?'

Paul Martiny didn't answer again and Scobell took his hands and pulled him upright. When he let go Paul fell back in the chair. The noise of the car was becoming clearer.

James Scobell was in his later fifties but he still weighed two hundred pounds, mostly muscle, and he picked Paul Martiny up almost casually. He had Paul's right arm on his own left shoulder and his right arm under Paul's right leg. He joined his right hand with Martiny's elbow. The fireman's lift, he thought, and grinned. His own left arm was free—he might need it. James Scobell was a left-handed man.

A car flashed its headlights once, then again. A pause, then the noise of an opening gate.

James Scobell with Martiny across his shoulder began to run down the drive to the gate and his car.

As he reached them he realized it hadn't gone well, not as he had hoped at all. The gate had been opened and that

162

was something, but the guard on it had not been immobilized. He was back in his gatehouse, the door locked behind him. The light was on behind heavy bars and he was using the telephone, talking hard. Mostly he was doing the talking but every now and then he would listen. He seemed to have made his connection already.

The Turks were standing uncertainly.

'Well?'

'He came out as you said but he thought too fast for us. He had a gun and he knew how to hold it too. You told us we mustn't kill him.'

'So?'

'He went backwards fast but he kept us covered. We had those other men's guns but you said——'

'I know.' James Scobell had dismissed it: it was one of those things. He put Martiny on his feet but still held him. 'Get this man in the back seat with you. Bring him round if you can but don't be rough.' He opened the glovebox and passed back a flask. 'Use this but not too much or too quickly.'

As they moved away a Turk said unhappily: 'I'm sorry there was a confusion. We——'

'We've got what we came for and that's all we need.'

He was lying but not ashamed to lie. What they needed now was a great deal of luck. The Turks were a race of varied virtues but fast thinking would hardly head the list and the two youngish men in the back were typical. In the Turkish quarter of Nicosia Angelides's power to act was nil, but the number of this car would be known and if that man at the gatehouse had passed it on Angelides could send orders by telephone. James Scobell smiled but without amusement: his brothers-in-law might not think of that. Which wasn't important but Angelides was. It would take him no time to confirm events once the news had arrived as it certainly would have.... A man had been snatched whom he'd meant to break, and snatched in the car of James Scobell with whom he had much unfinished business. James Scobell had a boat in Kyrenia harbour—that would be known as was everything else—and they still had a good sixteen miles to reach it. There'd be a telephone or perhaps even a radio ...

They were going to need luck, they were indeed.

He said nothing of this to his brothers-in-law. He respected their courage and generous loyalty but their judgement would not be a matter he valued.

When it came it came unexpectedly, not a police car alerted by short wave radio but three men in a jeep with the ugly blue berets. The driving mirror had shown them already but James Scobell had not been alarmed. A few miles ahead lay the Turkish enclave, blocking the pass through the hills to Kyrenia. Any tourist could pass it with waves and smiles but a Greek could only go through with protection and these men in blue berets provided the convoys. But not in the small hours of early morning. These men in the jeep were a routine patrol if the word was not ironically military.

He hadn't expected they'd try to stop him and when the loud-hailer blared he slowed reluctantly. He'd been driving fast for time was against him; he couldn't afford to lose minutes in argument but finally he slowed down and stopped. The jeep drew alongside, a soldier climbed out of it. He said in a strong northern European accent:

'Why you not stop to let us pass? I think you were making obstruction on purpose.'

Scobell's first emotion was simply annoyance. The jeep hadn't been flashing or blowing its horn but keeping a steady distance behind him. Till the loud-hailer had uttered its raucous bellow they'd been minding their wholly futile

164

business, three mercenaries driving a jeep by night, their object as ill-defined and untidy as the horrible clothes which disgraced their profession.

Scobell looked at the soldier with open distaste. He had all of the hireling's uneasy arrogance and he was acting outside his rights and knew it. . . . The country of Gustavus Adolphus, of Charles the Twelfth, once the scourge of Europe. And look at it now, or rather try not to. It struck attitudes which made one wince and it harboured a friendly country's deserters; it hired its army to a power which was not one, and if it could put your back up it did so.

As this overpaid peasant was trying to do. Nevertheless James Scobell's annoyance was now tinged with a certain apprehension. This idiot didn't matter: time did. He produced his passport and showed it politely.

'And the men in the back?'

'Two Turks and an Englishman.'

'Two Turks,' the corporal said suspiciously.

James Scobell could have blacked his eye with pleasure for the reaction had been both prompt and offensive. Turks were the troublemakers. No, they were not. They were no sort of match for Hellenic cunning, so when they were misused and cheated beyond the limits of a surprising patience they fell back on their ancestral remedy which was to defend what they held, by force if necessary. From time to time they used rather too much of it, but it was the only weapon they'd ever had. In James Scobell's sincere opinion to try to take it away with foreign troops was an outrage against all natural justice.

Scobell didn't say this, he didn't dare. This man might indeed be outside his rights unless he had some good reason to stop them, but if he searched them he'd have that reason at once. Three passengers out of four were

165

now armed and carrying arms was entirely illegal. This fool could arrest them with perfect propriety; he'd probably earn another stripe.

Scobell said again: 'Two Turks and an Englishman.'

'Their papers, then.'

'I don't think they're carrying them.'

The corporal went back to the two in the jeep who climbed out and unslung their carbines clumsily. They unslung them but they didn't yet point them. Scobell said to the Turks:

'How far to the roadblock?' He meant the northern one at the foot of the hills. There was another on the other side where the Turkish-held enclave stopped short of Kyrenia.

'Three or four hundred yards.'

'We'll risk it. Once through it they won't dare follow. That's certain.'

'And if they shoot before we're over?'

'I told you there was a risk. That's it.' Scobell looked at Paul Martiny uncertainly. The brandy had begun to revive him, he was sitting up straight, his eyes were open. 'Did you follow all that?'

'I followed a bit.'

'Then this rabble is an officious nuisance but they'll be very much more if they find we have guns. They could hold us and take us in. They'd love to. So I'm going to drive on and chance it.'

'Right.'

'You three at the back get your heads down hard.'

The corporal came back. 'Get out,' he said. 'All of you get out of the car.'

'Why should we get out?'

'Because I say so. You have obstructed us and insulted our flag.'

'Rubbish,' Scobell said. The engine was running. He
166

revved it up hard and let the clutch in. There was an instant cloud of pungent dust from the nearside tyre which was off the road. 'Get down,' he said.

They had done so.

'Lower.'

There was the crack of a carbine and then another. Neither shot came anywhere near the car. Paul said laughing:

'That wouldn't have done for the Duke.'

'What Duke?'

'Arthur Wellesley, Duke of Wellington, General.'

'You must explain the joke to me later on. But I'm delighted that you're with us again.'

At the roadblock they halted and the Turks talked rapidly. Their compatriots on the roadblock nodded, and as the car moved on again Scobell looked back. The barrier was out and manned. 'Okay for the moment,' he said. 'Let me think.'

He had reason to since they had lost some time and every minute could count till the police machine clicked. Even discounting radio they could telephone to Kyrenia and the name of his cabin cruiser was known. He had total faith in his other two friends: one would have brought his wife and two children—they'd be safely on the *Yellowstone* now—and the other would have collected Judie. Safely but there was that damnable telephone. If that man at the gate had been quickly believed, if bureaucracy had for once acted promptly, the *Yellowstone* could be the deadest of ducks. She might in fact be a loaded trap, a noose for the men who were trying to reach her.

Nevertheless the risk must be taken if the vessel were going to sail at all, and Scobell began to count his blessings. One had been the Turkish roadblock, since without it they'd have found no sanctuary, they'd have been held and

167

searched and arrested for certain. And another was Paul Martiny's recovery. He had ventured a joke when the shots had come past them, and though it had gone over Scobell's head a man who could jest under sudden gunfire was a man who was recovering strongly. James Scobell was still driving much faster than usual but for an instant he turned his head to Martiny. Paul was nipping from the brandy flask happily, smoking a cigarette with relish, chatting to the Turk who knew English. James Scobell nodded in real relief. If there were any sort of difficulty when the crisis came in Kyrenia harbour a man you would have to hold up or carry would at best slow down action and at worst might be fatal.

Scobell stopped the car in the street by the mosque, at the top of the hill with the harbour below. Between them and the pleasure boats at anchor was a warren of ancient fishermen's cottages. Many were now in other hands, converted with somewhat varying taste into summer retreats for men not fishermen. Scobell led the way through the lanes with confidence. 'If there's going to be trouble we don't want the car. To drive down in it would alert them at once, that is if there *is* a them to worry about. Perhaps there won't be, perhaps there will. We've been lucky twice but we mustn't push it.' By a block of new flats he halted suddenly. Here there was a gap in the buildings and the harbour was spread out below them. The restaurants on the quayside were shut but the street lights were on and Scobell pointed. 'The third to the left by the break in the railing. That's the *Yellowstone* and she looks all right.'

'How do you know?'

'Because she's showing a blue light as arranged. That means they're all aboard as planned—my family and your friend Mrs Shay.' He started to move but stopped dead in three steps. A big grey car had swung into the harbour, stopping just short of the *Yellowstone's* stern. Voices came up to them clear in the night, the inevitable excited chatter inseparable from any Greek action. Two men left the car and it drove away. They took up station at the *Yellowstone's* gangway.

'Those idiots playing at soldiers for money! But for them we'd have been at sea by now.'

Paul pointed at the men by the cruiser. They could see her by the harbour lights clearly but in the darkness they couldn't be seen themselves. 'Why don't they go on board?'

'Why should they? They can stop her sailing and they're waiting for us.' Scobell lit a cigar and frowned, frustrated. 'A clean sweep of the lot,' he said with anger. 'That's what they're playing for. Next move to us.'

The two Turks had begun to whisper together. The elder held one of the policemen's pistols and James Scobell said sharply: 'No.' He leant against a wall and thought, talking as much to himself as Paul. 'Those two by the boat are plainclothes men but it's a certainty they'll also be armed. My two are Turks and will be seen to be Turks; they haven't a chance of a sudden rush, they'd raise suspicion before they got near close quarters. I myself am also much too well-known.'

Martiny said: 'I may not be.'

'They'll have sent out some sort of description, though.'

'A good enough one? For two men who don't know me?'

Scobell looked at Martiny closely. He'd drunk most of a generous flask of brandy but he was a very long way still from being drunk. Dutch courage perhaps? James Scobell thought it wasn't. The police owed this man quite a sizeable debt: it would be a pleasure to try to exact a part of it even though all the odds were against him.

'I can guess what you're thinking,' Martiny told him.

169

Scobell noticed that he was standing easily, balanced on the balls of his feet. He'd been as near as made no difference to out but now he was Paul Martiny again. 'You think I'm a little drunk. I am not. But I've had enough to pretend to be.'

'What do you plan?'

Paul Martiny told him.

'I'm obliged to tell you you haven't much chance.'

'Have any of you three a better one?'

'No.'

'Then lend me a hat and a pair of dark glasses.'

He put them on and began to walk, down the slope to the quayside which skirted the harbour. He was walking unsteadily, rolling untidily, bawling an air from *Oklahoma*. He looked like the typical tourist in drink, or rather he sincerely hoped so. Tourists, he was thinking—the beaches. Girls in bikinis, the concrete jungle. The sun-trap as advertised—come and spend here. It was an arrogant sham on the brittle surface. Underneath there was naked civil war and the fact for the moment they'd somehow suppressed it didn't alter the inherent menace.

One of the police had his hand in his pocket but the other put out a restraining arm. Both of them stood quite still and watched Paul.

They were standing very near the edge and this was Martiny's only advantage. Once in his bedroom he'd hit a man and a fortunate blow had gone home on van Ruyden, but he knew nothing whatever of unarmed combat, especially against two men with arms. But what Scobell needed was twenty seconds, ten seconds to reach the *Yellowstone* and another ten to start her engine.

Paul Martiny reeled on, much closer now, and one of the policemen challenged him sharply.

'Who are you?'

170

'I'm God. And you're an angel. Good evening, angels. Good luck to you both.'

The second man said: 'You're disgustingly drunk.' The voice was contemptuous, scathingly Greek.

'I suppose I must be.'

'No doubt at all.'

Paul was almost up against the policemen when he managed a very convincing stagger. He went down on one knee and began to whimper, and one man put an arm out to help him. Paul held the hand as he rose and jerked viciously, thrusting out a foot as he did so. The man took two stumbling steps and fell. He fell into the sea with a curse. The other had taken a single step backwards, fumbling again to draw his pistol. Paul put his head down and butted his stomach. The man had his weapon out now and was waving it. He was waving it but, unbalanced, he dropped it. He went over into the water too. It had been slapstick against two men with guns but it was bold slapstick and the impertinence worked.

James Scobell had arrived in a powerful rush. He pulled Paul along the narrow gangplank, then threw off the painter and went below. There were four very long seconds. The engine started.

Paul was looking at the men in the harbour. One had managed to knock himself out in his fall and the other was holding his head above water. Both were Greeks and were thinking first of themselves. Put them anywhere near the sea and they did so, as the English who cruised in Greek ships had discovered.

The *Yellowstone* had begun to move, slowly at first as the twin screws stirred her, then gathering pace as she slipped from the quay. James Scobell had come back to the cockpit quietly.

'Lucky she started easily.'

171

'Very.'

'Naturally I'd told them to prime her.'

'You think of most things,' Paul Martiny said.

'I think of most things but I don't always act.' Scobell had taken the wheel but turned; he said to Paul Martiny respectfully: 'If you're ever without a job I could find you one.'

15

Van Ruyden was in appalling pain, all judgement destroyed in desperation. The blow on his eye had shattered him and he'd shot on the reflex of simple agony, not as he'd killed George Amyas, to plan. All plan had indeed been entirely forgotten, lost in the fog of his pain and the drug. He had ceased to think why he wanted it, that Report for which he had calmly killed; he had forgotten his grandfather's plan to use it, his own part in the political blackmail. All that was left was a blind compulsion. He had come here to get that Report. He would do so. He was Peter van Ruyden, he mustn't fail. He was also the last van Ruyden. He dare not.

And time was running out on him fast. He knew that he must get to a doctor, not only to stop the pain which was breaking him but also to save what was left of his eye. But if he did so the doctor would put him in hospital, and then they would fly him back to the States for the surgery he'd been warned was still necessary. Or suppose they just put him under and operated. Once unconscious he wouldn't be able to stop them, and to an American with American prejudices the thought of any major surgery outside his own country and therefore incompetent was more frightening than the thought of death. Besides, if they put him to bed he'd be helpless. He wouldn't be able to act and he had to.

He took the last of the Greek girl's nameless drug. It had lost its power to put him out but it was making him more lightheaded than ever. He took his motorbike and he drove to Judie's. He hadn't a plan, he was acting on reflex, a compulsion which drove him much harder than thought. Somehow he had to reach Judie Shay.

But through the pain and the driving desperation a small part of his mind was still thinking reasonably. Judie Shay had been guarded—she'd now be more so. Then if they forced him to shoot he would shoot it out.

He never did so because he was given no chance: James Scobell's Turkish friend had beaten him to it. Van Ruyden had left his bike down the road and was walking to Judie's house in the shadows. He had expected the guard to be reinforced and it seemed they had moved it from Judie's staircase. There were now two men on the outside gate and the pair of them were in battle order, or what passed for battle order with policemen. They had machine pistols hanging from slings round their necks and the lantern above the gate reflected on steel helmets which were a size too large. They hadn't yet noticed van Ruyden. He stopped. An American, he respected fire power.

A big black car came past him smoothly.

It stopped at the iron gate of the house and one of the policemen unslung his pistol. A middle-aged man got out collectedly and there seemed to be some sort of conference. In the light of the lantern van Ruyden could see, and the middle-aged man was displaying a paper. The policeman appeared to hesitate but the visitor's manner was quietly authoritative. Finally the sergeant nodded and the middle-aged man went through the gate.

As he walked up the drive he was smiling happily. He

was distinctly too old to indulge in rough stuff and he knew that he'd be outgunned in any case. But he had something much more effective than firearms; he had a letter on police headquarters' paper and signed with Asterios Angelides's name. The paper had been stolen that evening, and as for Mr Angel's signature, the elderly Turk had forged it himself. Forgery was his special gift, and more than once it had come in useful in the secret war his race was fighting.

So he walked up to Judie's staircase confidently. Later there'd be hue and cry but he wasn't concerned with that in the least. Like the brothers-in-law of James Scobell he'd have the protection of his own community where Angelides wouldn't be able to reach him and where he'd simply lie low till the heat had cooled. And his guess was that it would cool quite quickly. He had walked through Greek guards with a pass which was forged, and forged with the name of a senior policeman. Angelides would be looking an ass. No Levantine liked loss of face. He'd cool it.

Van Ruyden, in the darkness, waited, and after ten minutes the Turk came back. He had Judie Shay with him and was carrying her suitcase. When a sentry held out a book he signed it, then he wished the two men a good night in English. He climbed in the car with Judie and turned it.

As he did so van Ruyden slipped back to his motorbike, following the big black car to the harbour. By the route it was taking it could only be going there but it was going too fast for van Ruyden's two-stroke and he was pushing it to keep in touch. He was half-crazy with pain and the last of the drug and inevitably he made a mistake. On a corner he caught a handlebar and he pitched on his unprotected head.

175

He had no idea how long he had lain there but when he came to he had smashed his left hand. The fall on his head had sickened him but for the moment his hand dulled the greater pain.... This was total unreality, this wasn't his life, it was utter mirage. A dream, a sleepwalker's nightmare in hell. One hand was useless, his legs were putty.

He forced himself down to the harbour on foot.

There was a knot of men round an empty berth and van Ruyden crept closer along the wall. He could in fact have approached them openly and they wouldn't have paid the least attention. They were absorbed in a frenetic argument, shouting insult and recrimination. On the quay stood two dripping and sheepish figures and the others were abusing them furiously. It was all very Greek and got nothing done.

Van Ruyden crept nearer to hear what they said. A cabin cruiser called the *Yellowstone* had been allowed to escape under armed men's eyes, and the *Yellowstone* and what she held had been part of a deliberate trap which the man who was shouting loudest had baited. He had been going to sweep up the whole damned gang. Angelides was beside himself, a Greek who had had his nose pulled publicly.... James Scobell who had married a Turk and protected them, a thorn in the flesh of all decent men, had violently snatched a man called Martiny who'd cold-bloodedly murdered a policeman on duty and whom four others had almost succeeded in breaking. But these criminals would have had to run and the *Yellowstone* was their obvious target, especially when Scobell's wife and children were found to have gone on board her already. Then a woman called Shay, Martiny's mistress, is permitted to leave a guarded house in circumstances which were not yet clear but were certainly dereliction to duty. That would be sifted thoroughly later, but the trap had been set and

176

the mice had come to it. So they'd come and had stolen the cheese contemptuously. Two armed men had been thrown in the sea like sacks, who could consider themselves under close arrest and they'd be fortunate not to do time in prison. Asterios Angelides was waving his arms and swearing obscenely. The *Yellowstone* would make for Turkey and she had half an hour's start. Pursuit was hopeless.

Peter van Ruyden did not agree. The Report must be on the *Yellowstone* and as he saw it he still had an outside chance. One hand was useless but he could steer with an elbow. He also had a gun and would use it.

He knew what he needed and where to steal one.

Scobell was handling the *Yellowstone* confidently, slipping her out of the harbour to sea. She was a considerable but old-fashioned vessel, built in Trieste in the 1920s, something less than an ocean-going yacht but a good deal more than a coastal pleasure boat. He had taken out the original engine and replaced it with a reliable new one.

In the narrows between the old fort and the breakwater two patrol boats were moored stem to stern at the jetty. Scobell saw that Paul had noticed them and he waved a hand in cool dismissal. 'The Cyprus navy—don't give it a thought. One of them is unseaworthy and the crew of the other is only half trained. It needs two hours' notice to get her to sea and we can make eight knots without blowing the engine. A two-hour start would be more than enough even if one of them risked coming after us.'

'Where are we going?'

'To Turkey. To Anamur—it's nearest. It's all organized at the other end. There'll be a car for you and Mrs Shay and you have seats on the earliest flight from Ankara. You'll be in London in forty-eight hours at the worst. I'll

177

be following when I've settled the family.'

'I'm sorry,' Paul said. He sincerely meant it.

'You mean because I've had to leave Cyprus?' James Scobell's shrug was philosophical. 'It was a question of time till they ran me out. I told you I didn't play with politics but it's no use pretending they thought me an asset. I didn't meddle in local affairs directly but I did a great many things the Greeks disliked. I married a Turk which they considered an insult and I protected her people which was spit in their eye. They were bound to crack down on me sooner or later. Turkey for any Turk is home and my own is where my wife is living.'

'I don't know how to thank you.'

'Don't try.'

His wife came up from the cabin to speak to him and James Scobell translated easily. 'It seems Mrs Shay is a very bad sailor.' Outside the harbour it wasn't yet rough but there was a long slow swell and the boat was pitching. 'Would you like to go down and comfort her?'

'No.' Paul had spoken with a surprising emphasis. Of all men who might comfort Judie he himself was the last on earth to essay it. He wasn't the man Judie Shay would be wanting.

'Then I'll go down myself and do what I can.' An understanding man, Paul decided. Scobell pointed at the compass briskly. 'Keep her on north-west by north and don't change her speed unless you have to.'

When Scobell came back the weather had worsened, clouds scudding across the troubled moon. 'It's a very deceptive bit of sea. Round the coast it can be as calm as a pond but a mile or two out it can throw you about.'

'I suppose there's no danger?'

'Of foundering? None. She's a solid old tub who's seen worse than this, but I'm sorry for Mrs Shay below.'

178

'How long for the trip?'

'Eight hours to ten.' Scobell looked at the sky. 'I'd say nearer ten. This is going to get worse before it gets better.'

There was in fact quite a lively sea, not dangerous to the sturdy *Yellowstone* but Paul wouldn't have cared to be out in it in anything less well found and seaworthy.

Which made him all the more astonished when he saw or rather heard the speedboat. The whine of her outboard had come to him first. He pointed: Scobell followed his finger. For the moment the cloud had left the moon and the speedboat was almost as clear as in daylight.

'Lunatic,' Scobell said. 'A madman.' He put up his glasses and stared for some time, then he said in a very quiet voice indeed:

'The man driving her has a bandaged head.'

'What do we do?'

'We can't do a thing. He has the legs of us while he stays afloat. Which I'd put at a matter of minutes at most.'

The speedboat was coming up fast astern, not trying to ride the sea but fighting it. As often as not she was out of the water, her screw screaming protest, then falling back sickeningly.

'He'll break her back,' Scobell said unhappily.

He had a loudhailer out and had started to use it when the bullet knocked it out of his hand. 'Jesus,' he said but he didn't duck. He looked at Paul steering. 'I'll take her. Get down.'

'I don't think that's a good idea. He'll have several more shots and will probably use them. I'm expendable ballast but you're the seaman.'

Scobell didn't answer but nodded agreement. Van Ruyden was almost alongside now and once, as he misjudged a sea, Paul had to yaw to avoid a collision. A second

179

shot whipped across the cockpit but the speedboat had ridden away on a roller.

'He's got the tiller under an elbow, jammed. He's using the other hand to shoot.'

A third bullet clunked into the wooden hull.

'The petrol tank?' Paul Martiny asked.

'She's diesel—I'm not afraid of a fire. But she's wooden and there are people below. My wife, as it happens, and a couple of children. Also a Mrs Judie Shay.'

'Could a pistol do damage?'

'That's what I don't know.'

'You've a gun yourself.'

'Which I'll use if I have to. Alas that I'm a very poor shot.'

The speedboat was coming up again. They could see she was more than half awash, riding lower and moving a good deal more slowly, but van Ruyden could just control her still and he worked her in closer and raised his hand.

He fired twice and missed once. The second went home.

'He's much better than I thought he was or else he has the devil's luck.'

Scobell's wife put her head from the cabin and spoke. She seemed perfectly calm and was even smiling.

'She says he's holed us but above the waterline. Nobody's hurt and they're plugging the hole.' He looked at the bullet his wife had handed him. 'Forty-five, I should say, so on the odds a six-shooter. He's had five of them already. Good.'

He stood up from the cockpit's bench, a target.

Paul moved quickly to pull him down again, but the shot never came. There was no one to fire it. The worst of the seas they had met had caught them and the *Yellowstone*, without helm, went beam-on. Scobell jumped at the wheel and swung her straight but the roller had creamed

180

down in the cockpit, pouring into the cabin below them. Of the speedboat there wasn't a sign or trace.

James Scobell raised a hand in a sort of salute. 'I think that I'm going to miss that man. He had it all wrong but had something I haven't.' He pulled out a pistol and looked at it oddly. 'As it happens I'm a pretty fair shot.'

16

A week later James Scobell was in London, walking down the graceful steps of one of Pall Mall's smaller clubs. He was walking on air, all two hundred pounds of him, for his lunch had been superbly successful. His friend, the *éminence grise*, had listened, then commented in much the same terms as Scobell had once used in his private thinking. In the world which this man had once inhabited and which James Scobell himself still lived in it was an axiom to co-operate, even, when one could do so, with enemies, and mutual trust and over all things discretion were the essentials for any fruitful work. Both could be destroyed in an instant if it were known that an American diplomat had bribed an official in British Security. That seemed to be a fact, alas, and James Scobell had been holding the proof of it. He'd had reason himself why he'd never dare use it, so blackmail, which he hadn't suggested, would in any case have been out of the question, but the offer to destroy it quietly could only be called an act of faith, so it would be natural to show appreciation of an action from which they had both of them gained.

Then this prisoner in whom Scobell had an interest. The *éminence grise* had held up a hand. No, he didn't want any sort of detail, simply the name and the basic facts.

Naturally he would make no promises, nor would James Scobell expect them. But it wouldn't be unreasonable if this prisoner's wife were modestly hopeful. After all her husband had stolen that paper, and one didn't need a defence lawyer's skills to point out that if he hadn't done so a scandal would have been unavoidable. And as for his wife she had handed it over when another sort of criminal's wife might have thought along very different lines. Yes, this shouldn't be very hard to handle.

And later, over the brandy, they'd chatted. So Scobell had had to leave Cyprus? A pity. The *éminence grise* had been sympathetic. He knew most things about Scobell's background, and he wouldn't have left his home behind unless something had gone very badly wrong. The *éminence grise* hid an old grey smile. He'd seen certain reports from the island of Cyprus and he knew that Scobell had been walking a tightrope. Inevitably they would push him off it, if not this year then next year—he'd accepted the risk. Now he'd got away safely but could never go back. They'd sequestrate his house and sell it and a realist hardly needed to guess where the proceeds were going to find their way. The *éminence grise* didn't think that seemly. They had run Scobell out and he didn't blame them but it offended a very un-Greek sense of fairness that they should steal what he'd had to leave behind him.

Well, perhaps there were possibilities there as well as in the matter of Shay. There was this mining concession the island was touting and for the moment only London was interested. More accurately only one body was interested and the *éminence grise* had a seat on its Board.

He nodded but to Scobell said nothing. He couldn't arrange for Scobell's return but he thought he could fix that he wouldn't be robbed. He owed that to a very good colleague, a small price for the years of scrupulous dealing.

The *éminence grise* drank the last of his brandy. Scobell, he reflected, had several times beaten him but he'd never double crossed him once.

As he walked down the steps of the club Scobell smiled. He'd served fifteen years in this city he loved and he hadn't desired to lose their fruits, the trust, the respect, sometimes even the friendship. He had a pension coming up very soon and until it did he was still James Scobell. When they shelved him he had a wife he loved, a couple of children, sufficient money.

He began to whistle a sad little tune but he considered himself a happy man. In his trade that was very uncommon indeed.

The old man in the house in the high east Fifties was drinking a couple of bottles a day, much more than his doctor had told him he should if he wished to survive just a little time longer.

Julius van Ruyden did not. The formal news he'd received from Cyprus had been that Peter had taken a speedboat out, at night and in very uncertain weather, and that his rashness had cost him his life by drowning. These were the only hard facts vouchsafed him, but there'd been hints which had made the old man snarl since they'd been clearly designed to suppress more inquiry. Peter van Ruyden had been living, well, curiously, and there was some evidence that his private habits had been such as to impair his judgement.

The old man had snarled but he'd also acted, dispatching his private agent to Cyprus with instructions to smell out the proper story, and a week later he'd had the essentials on paper. His grandson had slipped into Cyprus and hidden. A man prominent in British Security had been discovered in a hotel pool after calling on an English lady
184

whose husband was now in an English prison. He'd been discovered by another Englishman who'd had contacts with the lady too and who later had been grilled by the police on suspicion of that and another murder. What had happened in that interrogation would never be known since the man had been snatched. An American who had married a Turk had disappeared in his boat with his wife and children and it was known whom this man had officially worked for. The English lady had vanished also, and all this had occurred on the very same night as Peter van Ruyden had stolen a speedboat. Those were the facts and the agent had found them: the story he couldn't piece fully together. There were a great many people with plenty to hide. There was a wall up and he couldn't pierce it.

The old man didn't blame him for that nor wish for more details he thought irrelevant. He had more than enough to make his judgement. His grandson had done his best and had died. He was a proper van Ruyden—he'd always known it.

Also the last one and that was final. The old man poured an enormous whisky. His plan had failed but that wasn't important, not now that his grandson had died with the failure. The last van Ruyden—that closed the books. The mines and the oil and the real estate, the railway, the steel and control of an airline. As an empire it had been worth fighting for but only as something to pass down smoothly. Great wealth could always be made and lost but an inheritance was essentially different. Now there was no one left to inherit.

The old man took another drink, working his wheelchair across the room. From a shelf of books he took down the biggest, his ancestor's family Bible in Dutch. On the fly leaf the names of succeeding van Ruydens were meticulously entered and dated. Under the name of Peter van

185

Ruyden he drew two firm black lines in indelible ink.

Judie Shay had listened to Scobell's phone call with spirits which had risen strongly. He hadn't spoken to her explicitly but his meaning had been perfectly clear. He'd been talking to the friend he'd mentioned and this friend, as expected, had shown his sympathy. As for Scobell and Judie Shay, there had once been a modest bet between them, a matter of twenty to one in fivers, and it was James Scobell's considered opinion that Mrs Shay would shortly be five pounds poorer. How shortly? He wasn't prepared to say since it depended on factors he couldn't control, including that a certain prisoner should continue to keep his record blameless. But provided this happened, as Scobell hoped it would, his friend had the means to fix the rest and he was confident he intended to use them. In the curious world which Scobell lived in men met their obligations promptly or they didn't have anything else to meet. She understood him? Excellent. Then the very best of luck to both of them.

Judie put the receiver down, aware of relief and of something more. The rules of her husband's world were immutable—when your man came out you were always there, to abandon him while inside was an outrage. Very well, she'd be there; she had always meant to be. What had happened in the interim was something to be forgotten. She'd do so.

Three years more, she thought, with moderate luck, and if it really broke her way it might be as little as two and a half. She'd get him back before they broke him and the waiting wouldn't break her either.

She looked at Paul's bowl of splendid roses. Flowers could say almost anything from 'Thank you for the entertainment' to 'I love you and I always shall'. These two

186

dozen were saying 'Thank you' gracefully. Thanks for the party, short as it was. Thank you and I understand. She was sorry about Paul Martiny but she wasn't in any way sorry for him. Paul had his life which she'd thought attractive, at any rate till her own resumed. And it wasn't attractive, it was violent and frightening, far worse than the life of a high-class thief.

Paul Martiny would not have agreed with her. He was sitting eating breakfast with Matty, more content with his lot than he'd been for years. He supposed that he shouldn't be feeling so—three men had died, though not at his instance, and a fourth, James Scobell, had lost his home. He ought to be feeling some twinge of conscience: instead he was eating a hearty breakfast. Why not? He was unusually hungry. He protected thieves to escape from boredom and the last few days had been far from that.

He had noticed that his wife was watching him and usually she read her newspaper. Men who claimed that they understood a woman were men whom Paul Martiny avoided, but he wasn't an insensitive man and he knew that what he now exuded was exciting to any woman. Happiness. He'd come back before from some girl in London and Matty had known the fact at once. She had known and she had been coolly indifferent. So she'd know that he'd been with a woman again but this time she wasn't indifferent. No. She was looking at him as a man, with interest. Her fine blue eyes hid a speculation.

He said suddenly: 'I've been neglecting you.'

'No.'

'You work pretty hard here. You've earned a holiday.'

'I work terribly hard at exactly nothing.'

'Then Nice?' he said. He knew she loved it. He had taken her there for their honeymoon and Matty had swallowed the south of France. He himself had always detested

187

it but that wasn't a matter which troubled him now.

'The baby?' she said.

'Has an excellent nurse.'

They hadn't sacked her, he remembered, smiling.

'I'll think about it.'

'I'll give you four minutes.'

'Sweeping me off my feet,' she said. It was banal but he could see she was flattered.

'I don't know about that. I'll book separate rooms.'

Matilda Martiny didn't answer.